D1010764

THE
TOAST

Also by Matt Marinovich

The Winter Girl
Strange Skies

THE TOAST

Matt Marinovich

ADAPTIVE BOOKS

An Imprint of Adaptive Studios • Los Angeles, CA

This is a work of fiction. Names, characters, places, and incidents either are the product of the author's imagination or are used fictitiously. Any resemblance to actual persons, living or dead, or locales is merely coincidental.

Copyright © 2018 Adaptive Studios
All rights reserved. No part of the publication may be reproduced, distributed, or transmitted in any form or by any means, including photocopying, recording, or other electronic or mechanical methods, without the prior written permission of the publisher, except in the case of brief quotations embodied in critical reviews and certain other noncommercial uses permitted by copyright law.

Visit us on the web at www.adaptivestudios.com

Library of Congress Cataloging in Publication Number: 2018942465
ISBN 978-1-945293-74-0
Ebook ISBN 978-1-945293-77-1

Printed in the United States of America.
Designed by Elyse J. Strongin, Neuwirth & Associates.

Adaptive Books
3733 Motor Avenue
Los Angeles, CA 90034

10 9 8 7 6 5 4 3 2 1

For Anna and Gracie

REBECCA

I've never understood why people find the last moments of a loved one's life so fascinating. Someone's uncle gets up early as usual, and then they find him lying by the old tractor near the barn. Or someone's little cousin was chasing a ball across the road, just like any other day. Or someone's husband turned to his wife in their car, just a few minutes before he died, and gave her a reassuring kiss, the same as all the other reassuring kisses he's ever given her. The wetness on her cheek almost instantly vanishing.

"I know how to change a tire," Rob said.

"This is why we have Triple A," I said. "We sit and wait. They change the tire."

But that was a white lie. It had lapsed months before. It had been crammed in a drawer near the sink, where all the other bills were banished. And when the drawer got too full, the bills were promptly relocated to the trash. It wasn't that we were broke. I just don't like veiled threats. *We've dutifully provided you with our services and now we expect payment.* I see the word *expect*, and it does something funny to me. It makes my heart start to beat a little faster. The back of my neck starts to perspire.

Don't expect anything of me. Then I guess I'm yours, bit by bit. Say nothing, and I'll talk to you all night. I've been talking to Rob for months. Sometimes I don't even turn the lights on. I can hear the faint ticking sound of the snow bothering the windows, some appliance in the kitchen fidgeting with itself, some temporary oversupply of energy. If you sit still long enough on a comfortable white couch, I'm fairly sure anyone would go insane and start asking their late husband questions. *How's it up there, Rob? Do you see me? Do you want to touch me? Is it cold? Do you feel anything?*

But most of all, I replay that last minute in the car. The oh fuck moment when you know you're going to have to deal with a little bit of bad luck. A flat tire. That unmistakable floppy flat tire sound flopping itself all the way down Smithtown Bypass, a road I never would have remembered if it weren't on the autopsy report.

I never saw the car that hit him. I'd been reapplying my lipstick in the mirror under the visor. I'd rolled my window down and shouted at him as he placed the jack near the left rear tire.

"You're not going to make me stand on the shoulder, are you?" I said.

I knew Rob would say yes, but he never got the chance to. The car that ran him over hit him at such a high rate of speed that his testicles ruptured. It's funny the things you concentrate on in an autopsy report, considering that almost every bone in his body was shattered.

I pursed my lips right after I asked that question, snapping shut my purse with the other hand, one of those silly clutches you walk around drunk with all night at a wedding. We'd skipped the rehearsal dinner the night before. His younger brother, Craig, was finally getting married, and we'd been stunned to get an invitation. I was even more stunned when Rob accepted it.

They'd despised each other for so many years, but then I suppose every damaged family member has a moment when they can't even remember how the bitterness started. A phone call is made. Or an invitation is sent. Somewhere in Africa, I read that tortured rape victims reconcile with their attackers, shed tears together in some courtroom, so I guess anything is possible.

Rob never called his younger brother. He just RSVP'd, like any other guest. Stuck the little card back in the envelope and slipped it into a mailbox. A few days before the wedding, he reminded me that we'd agreed to go and that he'd booked a motel in Stony Brook, Long Island.

"I'm working on a toast," he said.

■

I was driving east on Northern State, the sections of highway clacking pleasantly underneath the wheels. Rob was sitting in the passenger seat, staring at a piece of yellow paper in his hand. My husband was thirty-nine years old, and I was thirty-four. The next morning, at approximately 9:42 a.m., he'd be dead.

"Listen to this," he said. "Tell me what you think."

I reluctantly turned off the radio, and then there was nothing but a whistle of air through my window. As the late morning light scattered through the car, I glanced sideways and caught a glimpse of him frowning over the toast he'd written in honor of a brother I'd slept with three years before. I looked back at the road, then turned toward him again. Craig was still the handsomer one, I thought unkindly. But Rob was better in bed. And I was still in love with him after twelve years. I told myself that all the time.

"Hard to know where to start with these things," he said.

"Let her rip," I said.

"When I got the invitation to this wedding in the mail . . ."

"Snore."

"What do you suggest?" Rob said, his lips pursed.

"Turning around," I said. "Send some flowers?"

He looked down at the piece of paper in his hand and carefully folded it. He'd pressed his lips into a thin little line, which meant he was beginning to get pissed at me. His blue eyes glittered a bit. I always got a little thrill out of that moment, because I knew what a violent temper he had. He'd been working that out in therapy for years, dulling it with Prozac, Lunesta, Ambien, yoga, endless night jogs, meditation, more therapy, bad poetry, mindfulness, Cymbalta.

There were days I would've preferred a hard slap to hearing about a breakthrough in therapy. He was turning soft before my eyes. He was becoming the kind of guy who'd leave a half inch of toothpaste on my brush before he went to bed, and foam my coffee in the morning. He's become the kind of person who forgives a younger brother for sleeping with his wife. And then writes a fucking toast celebrating his marriage.

"I forgive you," Rob said.

"You what?"

"I forgive you for sleeping with Craig."

"I know, you've forgiven me many times. I'm up to my ears in forgiveness."

"And I forgive him too," he said. "Because I was a fucking bastard. I fucked up his life."

"He fucked up *your* life."

"I'm just not angry anymore," he said, smiling at me. "And there's nothing you can do about it."

I forced a smile, turned the radio back on just as he began to read the first line of his toast again. It was that song about cheap thrills that had been a hit one summer before. Just to annoy Rob, I began to sing it badly, hitting the steering wheel a little with the heel of my hand. I was thinking about the wedding, pictured myself flirting with some anonymous man in a suit, getting drunk at the Lagoon Bar after the reception. I'd visited the website of the Old Field Club the night before, spent an embarrassing amount of time playing a saccharine video of a bride and groom eyeing each other anxiously. Craig's fiancée, I realized, must have been rolling in cash. Because it sure wasn't the Venetian Club, where the caterer hadn't even shown up, where the DJ had vanished to do blow with a bridesmaid in his car, and where, to top it all off, I'd slept with Craig, an hour before a justice of the peace with bad breath and a stained white grizzle of beard had finally ushered Rob and me into matrimonial eternity.

"I'm hungry," I said to Rob, turning down the volume a bit. "How about you?"

■

The waitress had topped off our coffees at the Lake Grove Diner. It was one of those places that a son takes his aging mother out to lunch before checking her back into the nursing home. Pies going stale in a fluorescent refrigerated case. Rob was crossing out a word on that yellow piece of paper, then a sentence.

"I don't know where to begin," he said, looking straight into my eyes. He had beautiful blue eyes. The word *disarming* gets tossed around a lot these days, but they really were. For a moment, I forgot he was reading the toast.

"I guess," he said, quickly glancing down at the piece of paper again, "I could tell you the story of two brothers who were the worst of enemies. Who did things to each other that will never be forgotten . . ."

"Might want to get specific there," I said. "How you screwed the girl he was in love with back in college."

"It's a toast," Rob said. "It's about making peace. Moving on. Learning to be humble for once in my life."

Rob had a new shrink, but the words he'd stuffed into his head were the same ones. I didn't know why I had to be the one left with all the resentment. The spit can in the corner who remembered everything. I had this memory that was evidently now all mine. Rob at our dining room table, transferring funds online, talking in hushed tones to our lawyer, and then kissing me goodbye on a frigid winter night, car keys jangling in his hand. Our dog had been poisoned, and Rob had spent months planning his revenge.

"Do you remember," I said, waving away the waitress as she dolefully approached us with that lukewarm pitcher of coffee, "the night you left to beat him up?"

"I was out of control."

I reached across the table and grabbed Rob's hand.

"You drove around all night, and you came back."

Rob caught the eye of the waitress, scribbled an imaginary pen through the air for the check.

"What's your point?"

"He's still waiting for you to punish him. Maybe he even thinks that's why you've accepted the invitation. You've come to ruin everything, or worse."

"That's why this is going to bring him to tears," he said, nodding at the piece of paper. He folded it in two, then three. The waitress slipped him the check, and I finished the last of my coffee, noticing that my hand was trembling as I lifted the cup. I'd barely touched the burger I'd ordered and had left the fries just where they'd arrived, in a pale, oily heap. Rob stood up and kissed me on the top of my head, as if I were some lost child. At the moment, I wanted to strangle him, but when I look back on it now, my throat tightens up. I miss him so much I start to get dizzy. I stop wherever I am in the house, and sit down, waiting for the blood to stop rushing to my head.

As we left the diner, he was still holding the piece of paper, that toast he'd never give, like some kind of prayer, memorizing it when I wasn't looking, mumbling it as we left the diner, his eyes staring at some fixed distance as he recited it.

"I'm probably the last person you'd ever expect to hear these words from," he said, staring at me over the shining rooftop of the car. I pressed the key with my thumb and unlocked it.

"But I love you," he said. I stood there, a stand-in for Craig. "It's as simple as that."

■

Red flags. I'd dated enough guys to pick up on the warning signs after a couple of weeks. There was the chef who turned out to be an alcoholic, the investment banker who turned out to be married but texted me for months afterwards anyway. But other than that I'd considered myself relatively lucky. In college, I'd nearly gotten married to an all-around nice guy who'd gone prematurely gray, but I'd never regretted letting him go. The last time I had drunkenly checked up on all my exes on Facebook, the nice guy had a wife and kid somewhere in Indiana and was making soft cheeses.

But there was also a time in my life, say around eight years ago, that I was getting a little antsy. I'd show up at the family Thanksgiving and get that look from relatives as we shuffled around a table crammed with steaming side dishes. I'd just turned twenty-six, and I thought I was on pretty solid ground. I ran All Action Contracting in Manhasset, having taken over the business after my father died. It wasn't the sexiest job in the world, but it was close to home, and home was still my parents' place, where I was caring for my mother after she'd had a stroke. I felt I was doing some kind of small good in the world. Besides, our motto, "We Build Tomorrow," always made me feel optimistic about what lay ahead of me, as if walls could always be torn down to make way for a bright blue future. If I could knock down all the small mistakes I'd made in my life up to then, all the nowhere relationships and dead-end jobs, there was no reason my whole life might not change for the better.

But the weeks between Thanksgiving and Christmas can feel like a year when you're single. Even though I wouldn't admit it to myself, I was becoming more and more depressed, something inside of me getting colder, like a freezing black river running underneath a bright crust of snow. These are the details I still remember: my mother's eyes widening as she tried to repeat a word I'd shown her on a cue card. The mechanical, bowing Santa I'd playfully stuck on the front desk of the office, and the endless whirring sound it made. And a potential customer, asking me for an estimate. He had a friendly voice, but I remember that call distinctly because he paused at the very end of the call and asked me if I looked as pretty as I sounded. It was a cheesy line, but I was staring at the mechanical Santa twisting toward me for the thousandth time. He could have said just about anything that second week of December and it would have made me feel good.

"You're smiling, aren't you?" Rob Krider said, and I was. But I wiped it off my face real quick, as if he were watching me somehow. Knowing the Kriders, he probably was.

∎

I don't know how Rob had gotten hold of Craig's apartment keys.
I do remember that it was a two-bedroom, somewhere in Astoria.
As I walked through it with Rob, I guess the first red flag should
have been the story he was telling me. He'd just bought the place
in a short sale, and he wanted to start right in on renovations.

∎

"I think I'm into an open plan," he said, waving at the walls of the
railroad apartment. "Let's knock down all the walls so you could
roll a bowling ball from the rear to the front."

"But it's furnished," I said, reaching for a photograph that he
swiped away from me before I could see it. *And neatly furnished,*
I wanted to add. Nothing exceptionally expensive looking, but
someone had taken the time to assemble an Ikea coffee table and
cabinet. All the dishes and appliances were spotlessly clean.

"You never asked questions about who's on the other side of
short sale," Rob said, grinning at me knowingly. "Who knows
what happened to these people? Could be a thousand reasons they
fell behind on their mortgage."

"Well," I said, staring at flat-screen television and then an
unfinished game of Scrabble, the board still lying on the couch.
I remember the word *vixen,* for some reason. "We build tomorrow. . . ."

The rest of the walk-through was painless. He seemed almost
bored when I scratched out some figures and came up with the
estimate. About twice what I thought he'd pay. He looked well
dressed enough to afford it. Broad shouldered, put together,
a leather jacket that was a little too tight on him, but in that
crummy week before Christmas the smell of it made me strangely

happy. I liked the way he lightly touched his knuckles to each wall he wanted taken down. It was kind of manly. Authoritative. I liked the mysterious way he suddenly turned toward me as if he'd known me from somewhere before.

"I like space. No fucking walls. Except right here."

He was standing in front of the kitchen.

"I don't understand," I said.

"I want a wall right here."

We were standing in the kitchen doorway. Plates were still in the dish rack. Through the frosted glass of the cabinets I could see cereal, rice, cans of soup, all neatly put away.

"You can't wall this off," I said. "Because there would be no access."

"I don't like kitchens," he said, smiling at me. "I don't want to see it. Is that a problem?"

"Well, you could turn it into another room," I said. "Maybe it could be a study."

"All right," he said, folding his arms and looking at me playfully. "I'll be honest with you. I feel like something bad happened here."

"Here?" I said, trying to comprehend where he was coming from. "Like what?"

"I don't know," he said, rapping his knuckles thoughtfully on the table. "I'm just getting a bad vibe."

"Are you messing with me?" I said.

"Why would I do that?" he said, giving me a hurt look. "I'm just getting a bad feeling standing here. I never want to see this kitchen again."

I'd had wackier requests. A woman who wanted us to build a tiny McMansion for her two cats. A cheery-looking octogenarian who wanted his lake house to be submersible.

"Are you paying in cash?" I asked.

"Always," he said.

"What do you want to do with the refrigerator and stove?"

"Just leave them."

At this point, I was only sure of one thing. I was talking to a cute guy who was probably missing part of his frontal lobe, but at the very least I could do my ailing mother a favor by taking his money. We'd put up walls wherever he wanted.

"It's going to start to stink after about a week," I said, feeling compelled to point this out before I held my tongue for good.

"Perfect," he said excitedly. "I don't care what it costs," he said. "Just slip the invoice under the door when you're done. And I meant to ask . . ."

I stopped scribbling numbers on the piece of paper. I looked up at him.

"How would you feel about having a drink with me?"

"I don't know," I said. Then I thought, *Why not?* He definitely wasn't someone I'd date, but he was cute enough to fuck.

I told him I might be free sometime after Christmas.

"I was thinking now."

"I'm working now," I said. Maybe he wasn't missing some gray matter. *Maybe he's just up to something,* I thought. *Maybe he's just getting back at a girlfriend for cheating on him.* If that was the case, he had a pretty advanced sense of humor.

"So am I," he said, picking up his phone and glancing at a few texts before powering it off. "Just one?"

I didn't say yes. I followed him out of Craig's apartment, the same place we would later destroy and wall up and then charge him for. It was my first introduction to their vicious game, and the whole time I thought I was just being picked up.

It would take weeks for it all to get sorted out, and by then I'd be forced to admit to myself that I had a crush on Rob Krider. That afternoon we walked across the street, got a high table at a sports bar, and started drinking. There was only one time he apologized for rudely interrupting my life story as it all gushed out. He wanted to know if I could get my guys in there to start the demo immediately. He told me he'd love to take a few pictures before we left.

"The truth is that I want to surprise someone," he said.

"Who?" I said. I thought that this was the moment he'd come clean and tell me what he was really up to.

"Nobody important," he said, his blue eyes going distant suddenly. Maybe the beer buzz we'd caught, or the thought of those poor people on the other side of the short sale. "How about another drink?"

We had a couple of rounds. I'd been on enough dates with motormouths who barely asked me about myself, so I appreciated the fact that he genuinely seemed interested in my life. It was around the third drink when I selfishly realized I hadn't asked him much about himself.

"What about you?" I said, realizing that I was about to get sloppy drunk for the first time in weeks. "Are you as normal as you look? Any dark secrets?"

"I wish," he said, staring out the window at his brother's apartment. "Maybe I could invent something?"

Later, I would find out that Craig had come home from a weekend business trip and discovered his apartment completely demolished. It was our youngest employee, Rustem, a kid from Slovenia, who told us that there might be problem. He said that he was just finishing up the job when Craig let himself into the apartment. Rustem said Craig had physically assaulted him, and he showed me some bruises on his neck, but the kid was constantly getting into scrapes. He was always trying to get a little more money out of me, whether it was padding his hours, or telling me some sad story about a video game he couldn't afford. I didn't think much of it until Craig actually called.

He told me that I'd been scammed by his brother, who he referred to as a very sick individual who had convinced the super to make him a copy of his house keys.

"He just screwed you," Craig said. "Mentally, and probably physically too. How does it feel?"

"I don't know what you're talking about," I said. "But we'll get to the bottom of this."

I pictured him standing in his brand-new apartment. A straight shot from the east to west walls, and the kitchen and its evil spirits hidden away behind a three-quarter-inch panel of fireproof Sheetrock. Oh, and there had been one more request from Rob. Paint it all a neutral mental-hospital green. He said the color calmed him down.

"You're part of the game now," Craig said tersely. "And you have no idea what it even is."

■

Something you need to know: one act of vengeance doesn't make sense when you just consider it on its own.

Rob Krider had an apartment just outside Philadelphia. When I showed up at his sad little condo and yelled into his intercom, he buzzed me in and greeted me warmly, with a kiss, as if nothing had happened.

There was something wrong with his apartment. There was a mattress in the living room, no box spring. A laptop on the kitchen table, and pages of neatly scribbled notes. All his possessions had been stowed away in luggage that was lined up in the hallway.

"It's his turn," Rob said, nodding at the bags, all neatly tagged, ready for any destination. "I'm not taking any chances."

Before I could even ask him for the money he owed me in damages, he handed me an envelope of cash. He told me it was more than he owed me. I didn't need to count it.

"What's wrong with you?" I said.

I shouldn't have even sat there at the kitchen table, waiting for his answer. Maybe it was just a crush I had then, but it was enough to freeze me for the few seconds I should have stood up and walked away.

"You really want to know?" he said.

The funny thing is that he didn't explain it verbally. He sifted through some of the papers on the table until he found the one he was looking for. Then he handed it to me—several loose-leaf pages that had been neatly paper-clipped.

"We're up to number sixty-two," he said.

I studied the words and dates on the piece of paper, but they didn't make sense to me. After the number one, for instance, was written:

10/4/99 Craig starts it all. Shot taken.

Then

11/5/99 Craig gets stitches!

And then:

5/18/01 Craig poisons Rob.
11/25/03 Craig abduction and torture. Total cost $2,463.
3/3/04 Rob drugged and buried alive (twenty-four hours with
*   plastic straw; nearly suffocates).*

*4/3/06 Craig hires prostitute to sleep with Rob. Genital warts
    acquired.*
*5/1/06 Norovirus! (Balloons/stuffed animal sent to Craig's
    hospital room.)*
7/5/06 Rob's skull fracture/concussion. Ice on steps.

I ran my finger down all the other hideous, neatly written phrases
and dates: *accident, electrocution, fire, weekend revenge fuck, identity
theft, impersonation, happy birthday! sad news!, crazy neighbor. . . .*
The list stopped with

12/13/16 Reno job. Hide Craig's kitchen!

"You're a fucking psycho," I said, handing the list back to him.
"No," Rob said. "That would make it too easy. I love him. I
really do."
"Then why don't you just stop the game?"
"Just quit?" he said, looking at me as if I were crazy. "Let him
win?"
"Right," I said. "Why not?"
He looked as if he was suddenly sick to his stomach. His face
had turned pale. And everything I had liked about his face seemed
to change. The eyes became narrower, the lips thinner.
"I don't think I'm ready for that," he said. "Blame the old man,
I guess."
I didn't want to hear anymore. Or tell him that it was possible
to make healthy decisions in life. Later on, I'd understand the joy
of being malicious. How addictive the dark side of things was. I'd
blame it on his father, just like him.
At that moment, though, the crush, thankfully, was wearing off
fast. I was standing up. This was going to be the next story I'd tell

the next guy I met, and I was fairly sure he would be the normal one. Statistically, at least, I knew I had a pretty good chance.

"Take care of yourself," I told him, walking toward the door. He followed me down the stairs, across the parking lot, where wet snow had begun to fall. Shoving his hands in the pockets of his stiff Carhartt jacket and trying to smile at me as I got into the Jeep. He had calloused hands, the hands of someone who really worked for a living. He'd told me he picked up odd jobs on the East Coast, mostly carpentry and tile work. Now I knew it was all a front. He was like some kind of boutique assassin who only had one target, his own brother.

Later, an even bigger mindfuck: there were rules. They couldn't even kill each other; put each other out of their misery. Who had come up with this? That was the first question I'd ask him when I came driving back to his place, a day later. But I didn't know I was coming back then, that I'd even be intrigued by this brutal game.

"You need help," is what I said before driving off. As I drove away, I watched him grow smaller in the rearview, still standing there, a vague smile stamped on his face, as if he knew I was coming back.

Red flags? *Who doesn't have them?* was what I told myself a few days later. Besides, brothers always got over their differences eventually, no matter how intense their rivalry was. The other thing was that it horrified my friends when I told them about the list. The more they warned me to stay away, the more I realized I was going to give Rob another chance to explain. I'll admit it intrigued me.

A few nights later, I was back at his condo. We had fooled around on his mattress. I was sitting up, listening to the heat clank, my cheek resting against his knee.

"I'm going to be honest with you," he said.

"I'm listening," I said.

"I knew you might be into it," he said. "The moment I saw you."

I asked him how he knew, but I also stood up, tearing the sheet off the bed and wrapping myself in it. I was going to look for my clothes and leave one final time. My friends were right. The guy had serious problems.

"I'm really into mindfuckers," I said sarcastically.

"You have brothers?" he asked me. "Sisters?"

"Sister," I said.

"You get along?"

He reached out to grab the sheet, but I took a step away from him. I was standing over him, looking down at his naked body. He'd playfully placed a pillow over his groin and had the nerve to grin at me as if he really knew a thing or two about me.

"Yeah, we get along fine."

"When was the last time you spoke?"

"I don't know," I said. "Around Christmas. She lives in Seattle. Has a family."

"You're putting me to sleep," he said, stifling a fake yawn.

I told him the truth, right then and there.

"I don't have a dark side. I don't like fucking with people. I'm still pissed off about what you did to your brother."

He grabbed my ankle and then he wrestled me to the bed before I could get away. I heard myself scream with glee, and I was almost embarrassed by how happy I sounded. *Maybe you're a fucking liar,* I told myself. He was staring at me, too, waiting for me to realize it.

"I need a little help," he said, tracing his forefinger up my wrist, looking at me. "'Cause I think he might be a little smarter than me. And every turn has to be better than the last."

"You do need help," I said, letting him kiss my shoulder, my breasts, my stomach. Our bodies were intertwined in that strange way they always are when you're falling in love. His knee under my ass, my leg hooked around his waist. Then I was sitting on top of him and he was slowly lying back down again, my fingers curling into the spaces between his fingers.

"Are you in?" he said.

"You should see a shrink," I said.

He sighed, looked up at the ceiling.

"Guess I'll have to keep on looking. Find a girl who gets me."

That hurt, I'll admit. I pictured some vague replacement, black-haired like me, but younger. With a nice little dark side, just like he wanted.

"Where does he work?" I finally said.

"He teaches ESL at the YMCA in Park Slope. Loser. One-day classes or some shit like that."

"Ever thought about hiring a male stripper? He could have trouble with the language and just be sitting there at first. Then he suddenly starts taking it off. He could have a little boom box. Start grinding on him."

Rob had moved closer to me again; he was moving his hand up my leg, and then he was touching me.

"Holy shit," he said, showing me the wetness on his finger. "This is getting you wet."

"I'm getting wet because you're touching me, stupid," I said. But I wasn't sure. The thought that I might have a secret sadistic streak really frightened me.

"I'm never wrong," he said, reaching down between my legs again. "I know talent when I see it."

■

The night before my husband was killed, we stayed at a Best Value Inn on the Smithtown Bypass, 3.4 miles from the spot on the road where he would be hit by a car the next morning. It was a Friday night and there was hardly a soul around in Smithtown. The only thing that broke the silence was the occasional truck hitting its airbrakes on the highway.

I took a shower, wrapped a thin towel around my body, and walked into the room. Rob lay on one of the twin beds, still working on the toast. He looked up at me as I walked past him, sizing myself up in the small mirror that had been bolted to the wall near the microwave. I knew I looked tired, but I also took secret pleasure in the fact that my husband was staring at my backside instead of his humiliating speech.

"You're a goddess," he said.

"I'm a wreck," I said.

Without turning around, I watched him swing his legs off the bed. He walked up behind me, his chin resting on my left shoulder. He tugged the towel away from my hand, and then I was standing naked in front of him, my skin still a little pink from the steaming shower. He kissed my shoulder, my neck, tried to get at my mouth sideways. I don't know why I persisted in looking straight at the mirror instead of turning around. I felt like I was someone else watching us, and that turned me on. I arched my back a little and he moved closer to me, his thick fingers brushing up against the inside of my thigh, and then he was down on his knees, grabbing my ass with both hands, darting his tongue inside me.

"I love shitty motel rooms," I said. He rose to his feet, grabbed a fistful of my black hair, and made me look at the two of us in the mirror as he entered me. It was the first time we'd had sex in weeks, maybe a month, and I pulled out every little stop. I reached through my thighs and grabbed his balls, I told him how fucking good he felt, and then I felt him stop.

"You tell him that?" Rob said.

I shook my head, my heart sinking, my legs gone stiff. He was starting to go soft inside me. His brother would always be there, hands gripping my ass even harder. I'd told Rob every little detail because he'd threatened to leave me if I didn't.

"I never said a word to him when it happened," I said. I wished that would end it, but of course it wouldn't.

"When *it* happened?" he said, taking another step away from me. For a second, I thought he was going to hit me, just as he had the first time I'd confessed. "It's like some major event in your head now. You can't even say sex?"

"Sex. A fuck. A terrible mistake. Okay?"

"Do you masturbate about him? Do you think about him still?"

"No," I lied. I had once, or twice.

"You want to fuck him again, don't you?" he said. "You'd do it right at his wedding. You probably have it all worked out."

His voice was clotted up now with anger and humiliation. Me, I was crying, wiping the tears away as he finished. I remember he pulled out and sat at the foot of the bed, staring right through me.

"I'm sorry," he said.

"You know that's a lie," I said. "I'm yours forever."

I sat down next to him. I was the one who kissed his neck now, his perspiration already going cold, the muscle in his jaw tensing. I kissed his eyes. His eyelids. I wanted to believe, just for a second or two, that I could heal us. I felt like Rob's closed eyes were the place to start, my lips pressed against them.

"You're stuck with me," I said softly. "There's nothing you can do about it now."

■

I couldn't sleep that night. I wanted to wake Rob up several times, but I resisted the urge. He was passed out cold. I could barely hear him breathing. I lay on the other twin bed, turned on my side, and faced the window. You couldn't hear the traffic on the road over the sound of the air conditioner, but I could see the passing headlights slithering down the curtains. Early in the morning, sometime around three a.m., the neighbor next door stepped into his shower. I could hear the water drumming against the cheap plastic.

The wedding toast was sitting on the bedside table between us. I reached for the creased pieces of notepaper and walked into the bathroom. Flicked on the light and sat on the toilet, reading it. What he had finally settled on surprised me. It began:

I don't know where to begin. I guess I could tell you the story of two brothers who were the worst of enemies. Who did things to each other that will never be forgotten.

I could picture Rob standing beside me at a table covered with flowers at the Old Field house, the guests gradually quieting. Someone shushing the last of them, and then the word spreading fast that this was the older brother they'd heard so many rumors about. Rob's hand would be trembling as he held the piece of paper, doing his best to look his younger brother in the face. Craig would have that half smile on his face. I could picture him holding hands with his bride-to-be. His heart would be pumping twice as fast underneath his jacket, waiting for the worst. The Kriders always knocked it out of the park when it came to the worst.

As soon as they could walk, they had learned that nothing was as precious as a grudge. It was more valuable than any precious stone because it only belonged to you. Turning it to revenge was an art their father had taught them with such great care. He had even left them a surprising amount of money, so that they could dedicate themselves to the game and not worry about actual jobs.

I think Craig would probably agree that our late father would not approve of this moment. But he's rotting in hell somewhere, and I'm standing in a kind of heaven for a moment. Because I realize something so simple it must seem stupid to everyone sitting here. I love my little brother and I want him to be happy. I'm sorry it's taken me so many years to say that.

I looked at the last page of the toast, but all those lines had been crossed out. In the end, he had decided to leave it short and sweet. I could picture him standing there, looking down and putting the folded toast back into his jacket pocket. The guests, used to weddings where brothers would endlessly embarrass each other with funny anecdotes, would be nervously sliding their dress shoes on the parquet, trying not to cough in the silence. But then all my husband would have to do was raise a glass and look vulnerable. They'd smile at each other from across the room and everyone would clap.

I'd only seen Craig truly happy once, and his face had looked like a mess, splotches of blood spreading across his pale skin like some kind of allergic reaction. It was part of the reason I was attracted to him. When he let his guard down, he looked like someone who needed saving. I guess I've always had a soft spot for guys like that.

The toast my husband had written wasn't bad for someone who couldn't write. He had struggled with it all day, so who was I to edit it, make him sound less stilted? Having finished it, my husband had been able to fall asleep like a baby, oblivious to all the nagging little voices that had tortured him for so long. A weight had really been lifted.

I folded the pages again, flushed the toilet just in case he was listening to me in the room. I walked toward the bed and put the toast back down on the bedside table. A sickly blue morning light had begun to cling to the carpet and walls.

I climbed into the bed next to my husband and asked him gently, like all envious insomniacs, if he was really sleeping.

"Yeah," he said, his eyelids twitching as he dreamed. "We'll be there soon. It's only ten miles away."

"Sure," I said, covering the back of his hand with my palm and squeezing.

"No turning back," he said.

CRAIG

*I*n the last fall he was alive, the six acres my father owned in western Pennsylvania actually looked sort of beautiful, though it was going to pieces. Even the lake had dried up. Still, the fading sunlight in the yellow oak leaves, the smell of real wood smoke from some neighbor's chimney, made it feel somehow quaint. I was thirteen that year. Rob was sixteen.

Sometimes we'd hear the laughter from young lovers or newly-weds who had come up to Rolling Hills Resort. One of its hiking trails bordered my father's property, which I found a little cruel. Every other day or so, especially in the fall, he had to listen to couples who were still in love, their tender voices carrying in the wind like a curse meant only for him. He'd walked through those same woods with my mother, and been in love, just like them. And then she'd simply fallen in love with another man.

It made so little sense to him, and it made him so angry, that it was never once discussed. Still, when he heard the voices of another honeymooning couple echoing through the woods, you could see the muscle in his cheek tense up. It was like he was listening to the past, and those happy voices made him so miserable that he filled the windows of his bedroom with foam that turned a jaundiced yellow.

Sure, Dad should have blown his brains out the day my mother left him, but that would've made it too easy on everyone. Instead he waited for her to drop us off for one of our court-appointed weekend visits. He'd waited at the end of his driveway for her to drop us off— then BANG.

Not too many weeks before the suicide, he told me that he was waiting for the day one of those couples blundered across his property line. He said he'd shoot them dead. When I looked at him in disbelief, he'd just given me a quick smile and tilted his head with satisfaction.

"Called trespassing, Craig," he'd say. "Let's hope they don't force my hand."

I didn't have the courage to talk him out of his obsession with those couples, but once I nailed my own handwritten pages to a few trees, warning them to keep away. My father found them and tore them down. He didn't replace them with a single no-trespassing sign. As far as he was concerned, if someone stumbled across his property line, it was fate.

When our mother dropped us off, my father never greeted us. He was always standing by the house, with his back toward us, tearing apart something in the garage, or standing sideways and listening intently, as if a pair of the Penn Hills honeymooners, calling sweetly to each other in the distance, were about to make their fatal mistake. It was like we weren't even there, until we were standing just a foot away from him. He didn't want a hug or a kiss, and he'd get red-faced mad if we ever told him we missed him. His children paled in comparison to the person he really wanted to see, and she put the car into reverse almost as soon as we stepped out.

The best way to start with him was to walk right by him and wait for whatever mood he was in to subside. Staying on the right side of his temper was exhausting. We ate dinner, some sliced deli meats he'd usually picked up at the nearest supermarket, while watching the same DVD on the TV, a rear-projection monstrosity he'd gotten a discount on because it was a floor model. He preferred the movie *Blood Creek*, an Australian horror film that ended in the murder of four innocent hikers. It had given me terrible nightmares, a fact I reported to my mother and then realized my mistake. If my father knew you were bothered by something, he'd dig at it until you really began to squirm. When we were terrified, when our eyes opened wide and stared at him unblinking, that's when he always truly started to relax.

He didn't know a thing about deer hunting, but because our mother had left him for a vegetarian and an animal lover, he made it a point to buy us three Remington .30-06s and even two tree stands from Cabela's that he'd put together the wrong way. Every Saturday in the fall, we'd put on our camouflage gear and follow him into the woods.

"You aim ten inches to the right of its chest," he whispered to me one afternoon. He was referring to the whitetail we'd never actually ever see. About forty yards away, Rob was sitting in a tree stand by himself, so bored by watching dead leaves fluttering past him that I think he had fallen asleep. I was stuck in the tree stand with my father, one of those two-person deals that had a railing you could rest your gun on and two collapsible chairs. Anxiety always bubbled up in my chest after a few minutes of being next to him, so the prospect of six more hours trapped there was making me feel a little overwhelmed. I wished he'd picked Rob instead of me, but my father was not stupid. He realized how much his oldest son already disliked him.

"You hear that crackling sound?" my father said. "We're going to have company pretty soon. Keep your eyes peeled."

I didn't want to tell him it was probably some hikers from the resort, or a nearby woodchuck.

"Does he sleep over?" my father said, staring into the distance.

He meant my mother's boyfriend. "Yeah, he sleeps over," I wanted to say. I heard my mother and her new boyfriend having sex even when they were trying their best to be quiet.

"Nah," I said. "I don't think she's that into him."

"I'm not taking her back, even if she comes crawling on her knees," my father said, clearing some spit deep in his mouth and hawking it out onto the ground. I could see the eye of his saliva, just where it landed, an eye as dead as his eyes, staring right back at us.

I was suppressing a very intense need to burst out laughing. There were times his delusions made me feel sorry for him, and then there were times like this, when the image of my mom crawling on her knees up his ruined driveway struck me as so funny I couldn't wait to share it with Rob, asleep in the other tree stand.

I got control of myself. Bit my lips. Felt a single joyous tear slip down my cheek. But the day was just beginning. No deer ever crossed our path. Not even hikers from the lodge that he might pick off instead. Even the woodchucks and squirrels vanished without a trace. The leaves stopped falling. For a moment, I convinced myself I was stuck in time, and would be trapped forever with my unhappy father in a tree stand. And my older brother, the only person in the world I truly loved then, would always be slumped over, head resting against the railing of his tree stand, motionless.

Rob was asleep.

"It's getting cold, Dad," I said finally, envious that my brother was dreaming while I was stuck in the miserable present with my father, listening to the liquid slosh in the flask every time he took a sip.

I really had to summon up my courage just to utter those words. It was already starting to get dark, too dark for sure to see some whitetail that didn't even exist. It should all have been obvious to him. But for an hour, he had been angrily staring at his oldest son, peacefully sleeping. At first it had just seemed to gnaw at him, the way all acts of disrespect got under his skin. He took another sip of warm vodka and tucked the flask back into his jacket. He resumed staring at Rob. I began to get a little worried, but I knew that if I shouted out my brother's name and he groggily woke up, it would have made my father even more incensed. Dad was always coming up with sadistic games in his head, playing us off each other. It might have started as a lark, but then he realized it was an even better distraction than *Blood Creek*.

"How about we wake him up?" my father slurred under his breath, his eyes widening as if he were truly being playful instead of just plain sadistic. And then he tapped the butt of my gun. "Let's see if that rifle works."

I knew that once he got an idea in his head, it would only get stronger, and I tried to think of some way I could knock him off track.

"I'm hungry, Dad," I said. "Can we go back?"

"Aim at the trunk of the tree," my father said, clasping one of his heavy hands around mine, forcing me to grip the gun. "You'll miss him by a mile."

"No," I said. "He'll never forgive me."

Even then, I have to hand it to myself, I knew exactly what was at stake. I was trembling too. My whole body shook like I'd been trapped inside a meat locker for a day.

"Take the shot," my father said, wiping his mouth. His blue eyes had become clearer; his weathered skin seemed to almost shine, and some ruddy color had appeared in his cadaverous face.

"Dad," I said.

"Wake that fucker up."

I looked up at him helplessly, but events had already been set in motion. He cupped the back of my neck with his hand, forced my head down until my eye was pressed painfully against the scope.

I've always felt that there's a connection between brothers that goes beyond biology. They can sense things in the air, maybe halfway around the world. An outside threat to one can be perceived by the other thousands of miles away, even if they're standing in the middle of a kitchen somewhere, pouring a glass of orange juice. And a threat from one to the other? It's instant.

That's why I think Rob started to wake up, even before I took the shot. It was almost as if I'd called out his name to warn him, but I hadn't. At least not out loud.

My father would later tell him that he had been urgently whispering in my ear, asking me what the hell I was doing. But I remember exactly what my father was whispering:

"Do it now," my father said. "He's going to piss his pants."

"He's going to kill me," I said.

"Squeeze the trigger, you little faggot."

I fired before my brother could turn and scream at me, and before my father could say another word about what a little fairy I was.

A piece of bark flew off the tree that Rob was perched on, ten inches below his right boot. He launched himself into space, grabbing the railing of the tree stand and then swinging once into the air before landing in a heap on the ground. He came running at us at full speed, so furious at me that he wasn't even aware that he'd broken his ankle in the fall.

My father watched his oldest son with growing pleasure as he clambered up our tree stand faster than any black bear could've. I didn't protest as he ripped me from my seat and dragged me to the ground, my father coaching him from above as he rained his fists down on my head.

"Now we're having fun, boys!" my father shouted. "I knew it was just a matter of time."

REBECCA

*M*y phone's alarm went off at 7:45, and I hit snooze. Rob found my hand, held it tight, and then brought it up to his heart. I thought he'd fallen asleep like that, but suddenly he made me reach down so I could feel how hard he was. He turned over, kissed my neck and shoulder. He lay on top of me and pulled the ratty blanket over his shoulders, covering both of us.

At first it was almost perfect. I brought my mouth close to his ear, but didn't say a word. My chin dug into his shoulder now as he pushed inside me. But as soon as I moaned, I felt him freeze. I opened my eyes and saw that he was staring at me hatefully.

"How many times did he fuck you?" he said.

He's never going to get over it, I was telling myself. *Why do you stay?*

"Once," I said, feeling nauseous. "I'm not going through this again."

"You're going to go through it as many times as I want."

I tried to wriggle away from him. It was all ruined again.

"Get off," I said.

I tried to push him off, my hands balled into fists. The last thing I was going to do was say sorry again. The word meant nothing to him.

"I'm going home," I said. "You can go fuck your brother. Why don't you do it in front of everyone after you read your toast?"

He rolled onto his side, and I marched angrily into the bathroom, slamming the door. If I said nothing at all, at least I couldn't make it worse.

I could hear him getting dressed for the wedding in silence, imagined him tightening the knot of a blue silk tie in the mirror. He'd worn the same tie to every major ceremony in his life, funerals and weddings, so there was no point in buying a new one. It had belonged to his father, of course.

I twisted the shower knob and stood there under the thin stream of water, telling myself that things always seemed darkest before dawn, or some kind of garbage like that. When I walked out of the bathroom with a towel around me, twenty minutes later, he was sitting in an armchair by the window with his hands on his knees, the air conditioner rattling next to him.

"Hey, beautiful," he said softly.

That was Rob. Anger vanishing as if it had never been there to begin with. It was disconcerting, to say the least.

"Hey," I said doubtfully.

On the dresser table, his cell phone was ringing. I watched him grab it.

"Rob?" I heard Craig say tentatively on the other end. He sounded nervous. They weren't used to simple, innocuous communications that weren't prelude to something awful.

"The big day," Rob said.

"The ceremony is at eleven," Craig said. "You have the directions?"

"The Old Field Club. Yeah, I got it all plugged in. We're only ten miles away."

I stood near the bathroom door, a few last coils of steam snaking out and disappearing. I was listening to every word.

"Did you both make it?" Craig asked.

Funny how that little question seemed to get Rob instantly bent out of shape. I thought of his therapist, sending him back home every week with a new phrase to work on: *I love you. I forgive you. I love myself. I love forgiving you.* There should have been a laminated card with those words in his pocket, because he sure looked like he needed them now.

"Yeah, we're both here," Rob said.

I could just make out Craig's faint voice.

"It'll be great to see you," Craig said. "I've got to run."

"Craig?" Rob said, and I wondered if his little brother had already hung up, or if he was waiting for Rob to give him a hint of what was to come, bad or good. I was certain that Craig's heart would be in his throat, wondering if it was now that some awful threat would finally be whispered.

"See you, baby bro," Rob finally said, ending the call. He looked up at me with that unreadable poker face.

"Are we all good?" I said, a few drops of water from my wet hair falling on the carpet.

"Nothing but good," Rob said. "It's going to be a bright happy day."

I watched him stand up and straighten his tie in the mirror again. If it was an act, it was a pretty good act.

"I should get ready," I said.

"You should," he said, giving me a quick smile and then walking over to the bedside table where the three crumpled pages of the toast were. Craig's redemption and his, sitting right there. He folded the paper and tucked it into his jacket pocket.

"So this is all about forgiveness still?" I said. "No change of plan?"

"Why would there be a change of plan?" he said, moving closer to me. In the mirror I could see the back of his jacket, the thin seam of blue tie he hadn't quite tucked in underneath the collar. I did that for him now as he kissed my neck.

"Sounds great," I said, "But what about Plan B?"

"Plan B is always in effect," he said.

"I love you."

"Can you get dressed?" he said, a little impatiently. "You know how us Kriders are. Everything has to go like clockwork."

■

We needed gas. I remember we pulled into a BP about a mile away from the motel. I was hung up on the failed sex we'd just had, wondering if it was going to go that way forever. A half-dozen therapists had sanded the edges off Rob, but the one place he couldn't forgive me was in bed. It would always start out normally, his hands cupped under my ass as he kissed my neck, just like the old Rob, and I'd breathe into his ear, moan a little, because he loved that. Then I'd look up into his blue eyes, wide open, and he wasn't there. He was stuck in time again, and I was betraying him all over again. The only way he could finish was to momentarily pretend he was his vindictive little shit of a brother. It surely would've made Craig Krider smile.

"Water, coffee, anything?" Rob asked, climbing out of the car.

"I'm good," I said. I was staring into the side-view mirror, some minivan parked near the air pump, a red-and-yellow kayak strapped to the roof. It was the kind of day you can feel the humidity and heat right away and it wasn't even ten a.m.

Nine thirty-eight, actually. There's security camera footage of Rob in the gas station. They checked it after he was killed to see if anyone was following him. But it's just Rob, grabbing a bottled water, making himself a cup of coffee, smiling at the clerk. Nobody appears in any of the other frames. Nobody standing in a hooded sweatshirt, watching him from one of the aisles. No one standing outside the doorway. No one standing near my car.

I was the only other camera, and like most people before a tragic event, I was doing a terrible job of recording anything of importance. In fact, I flipped down the visor and started to touch up my makeup. I'd stopped paying attention to the dad inflating the tires of his minivan, which is ironic, because at that very moment, our rear left tire was rapidly leaking air. The detective would later say that it had been timed perfectly. Someone had slashed it just before we walked through the front door of the motel, probably with a box cutter, the detective said. It would take a little over ten minutes for the tire to go completely flat.

I do remember a gas truck pulling in, the sun reflecting off its stainless steel, the cab shuddering to a stop as the driver turned the engine off. It obstructed my view of the highway, which wouldn't have mattered to me, but anybody who had been following us from the motel could have pulled up on the other side of the truck and been hidden from view. They would've had a clear view of the Maple Road exit, and would've easily been able to follow us as we pulled back onto the bypass.

Before Rob walked back to the car, I'd flipped the visor back up. I didn't want him to see me primping for the ceremony. I didn't want him to think I cared at all how I looked. I heard him wind the gas cap shut, smack the fuel door shut.

"Want a sip?" he said, settling into the car again. I took the coffee from his hand, allowed myself a lukewarm taste. I was staring at some wood chips that had been poured around a sad little hedge, and then in the distance, across Maple Road, two children, barely visible, chasing each other across a lawn with Day-Glo water guns.

I was suddenly, unexplainably happy, and I turned to Rob and kissed him on the mouth. Maybe there was a chance we'd finally be able to move on. Maybe this was the closure he needed before he could sweep the last bit of darkness out of his heart.

"I'm feeling better about this," I said. "I think you can really pull it off."

"Pull what off?" he said, as if he had no idea what I was talking about.

"Forgiveness," I said.

"What the hell are you talking about?"

"Rob?"

"I'm kidding," he said. "It's all about moving on."

He gave my hand a quick, reassuring squeeze, but this time he sounded much more unenthusiastic. He took the cup of coffee back from me and took a sip, staring at something in the rearview mirror.

"We'll find another way to get your adrenaline going," I said, trying to be helpful. "White-water rafting. Ice climbing. Group sex."

"We're going to be late," he said, smiling at me and turning the key in the ignition. "How about we get this over with?"

■

Seven minutes later, it happened.

"Someone must have slashed the tire," Rob said.

It must have been ten a.m. I could see the perspiration running down his back, his dress shirt plastered to his back. He popped open the truck, tossed aside some old sandy towels, and found the jack and the spare. The spare, he figured, would easily get us to the wedding at the Old Field Club in Setauket. It was only ten miles away.

He placed the jack near the wheel and crouched next to the car, one hand resting against the rear window for balance. I could hear him start to crank up the jack, I shouted at him through the open window.

"You're not going to make me get out of the car, are you?"

He didn't answer me, because he was looking at the tire again and that little inch-long welt where it had been slashed. The last of the air had escaped and the rim had now met the road. The whole car was now tilting about six inches off-center. I flipped the visor down and reapplied some lipstick in the mirror.

You want to hear something funny?

I was going to tell him to be careful.

I heard a sickening *thunk*. No, more like a small explosion. And then my husband flipping through the air, because that's how high the impact had thrown him. I didn't hear him crash to the ground because I was already screaming.

■

He wasn't instantly killed. Yes, his body was too absurdly ruined to even feel any pain. But he was conscious less than a minute by my guess, definitely more than thirty seconds. He was lying in the exact middle of the highway, his head facing his own car, one arm slowly reaching backward. He was about thirty yards down the road, the tire jack still under the left rear right wheel. One of his dress shoes was sitting on the asphalt, the laces still tied. Drivers were leaning on their horns as they passed me, as if my husband had chosen this spot on purpose, half his jaw missing, his collapsed lung deflating.

It was so surreal that the most terrible thing almost, almost happened. I thought I was going to laugh. Because it had to be part of the game. He'd built a mannequin that looked just like him and he was going to climb into the car in a second and take a cell photo of my shocked face.

But then he was still there. Turning on his side and then lying on his back one final time. His arms stretched out behind his head as if he were surrendering to the empty blue sky.

His eyes would roll back into his head and his pupils would grow fixed before I could even take one step toward him.

I didn't want to move. To move an inch, to even reach for the door handle, to even say his name would make it real. Cars had slowed to a stop all around me. Someone was tapping on my window.

I turned toward the visor and looked into the mirror. I pursed my mouth and applied more lipstick, the sounds of strangers banging on all the windows now. Asking if I was all right. Of course I was. It was only a flat tire. We didn't need any help. Rob was always good with his hands. Practical things. I had a feeling we'd even be early for the ceremony.

My cell phone was ringing, right on cue. It was Craig. He kept on calling for an hour after that. It's all there, preserved on my call activity log: 9:57 a.m., 9:59 a.m., 10:02 a.m., 10:04 a.m.

The prick, checking in on me, wanting to hear the grief pouring out of me. A scream maybe. When I answered, half an hour later, I was sitting in some dry grass on the side of the road, waving off a paramedic.

"Why?" I asked him.

I ended the call before he could answer and hugged myself. I was shivering and it must have been eighty degrees.

CRAIG

I'll tell you right where I was when Rebecca called. I was standing in the dining hall of the Old Field Club, talking with the caterer about roasted duck wontons. I held up a finger and walked outside. There were guests everywhere, and the only place I could go to take the call in private was under the trellis where I would be getting married to Laura in an hour. I stood under it, staring at the calm blue water of the creek, swans gliding toward the reeds.

"What's going on?" I said.

"Rob's dead," she said. Behind her I could hear a woman laughing, then a man shouting something unintelligible. I knew it was a joke. Something to throw me off my game at the last minute. Vintage Krider.

"Well, put him on some ice and get down here," I said. "Because the ceremony starts . . ."

I looked at my watch, saw one of my groomsmen walking toward me in a suit that looked a size too small for him.

"The ceremony starts in forty-five minutes—" I told her, but she'd already hung up. Kerry had reached me, hung over but smiling.

"So this is it," he said. "Any second thoughts, I'm your man."

"You're stepping on the rose petals," I said, pointing to the scattered flowers under his feet.

Later, a detective would ask him to recount the exact conversation we had the moment I got off the phone. Being hung over, Kerry would get it all wrong anyway. He would tell the detective I looked distraught, that my face looked pale, and that he would follow me as I walked toward the creek and, placing my hands on my knees, tried to throw up as neatly as possible.

That was all after the second call. Two or three minutes later. This time Rebecca said nothing. And then she made the strangest noise, as if she was gently laughing. I was going to laugh along with her when I realized the sound had become steady sobbing. I heard the phone slap on the floor, then a dozen other voices. It wasn't Rebecca who finally picked up the phone in the waiting room at St. Catherine's, it was just some strange man.

"Hey," he said. "She's going to have to call you back. She's going to pieces, all right. The doctors just gave her some bad news."

I still didn't believe it, even after I went pale, and got sick, and watched the swans paddle away from me.

"What's going on?" Kerry asked me. He sounded like a frightened girl. But when I turned around and saw the sunlight shining all over his brand-new suit, saw his combed wet hair, and then allowed myself the whole panorama of my fucking perfect day: two bridesmaids wearing an awful shade of pink, sneaking a cigarette like teenagers, my wife's parents arm in arm, walking toward me with pinched, expectant faces. When I saw all of this, I told myself that nothing had happened at all.

"Wrong number," I said to Kerry. I gripped his shoulder, turned him around. At that very moment, I knew for a fact that my brother was lying on a gurney, dead, his eyes open and gray and waxy. A brother can feel these things and the dread that comes with it, like some tsunami warning that blips on some poor fuck's phone and warns them they have eight minutes to get to higher ground. In fact, my phone was ringing again, and I turned toward Kerry and shook my head, turning off my phone.

"Never fails," I said.

"Guess you're just as hung over as I am," he said.

"Good as new," I said, wiping my mouth with the back of my hand. Laura's father and mother seemed to get smaller and smaller the closer they got to me, like some kind of optical illusion.

"Man of the hour," the father warbled.

"That's me," I said loudly, though I didn't have to, because his hearing aid was already in.

"I'm not supposed to tell you this," he said, pulling me aside. "But she's going to knock you off your feet when you see her."

REBECCA

I *have to remember everything,* I told myself. Otherwise, how would I ever tell the story? The details are always important, aren't they?

One of the doctors said that the porters had brought my husband down to the mortuary, and that I could spend as much time as I wanted with him there. Of course I had to brace myself. Rob would never have forgiven me if I had walked away from the hard part.

The doctor walked me to the elevator and we entered it together. There was blood all over my dress. It had soaked in and dried. The doctor pressed a button and we descended. The elevator must have been eight feet long, all stainless steel. Long enough to fit a body on a gurney.

"We have a chapel as well," the doctor said.

He looked so young that for a moment I thought he wasn't real. That he was an actor playing a doctor. Along those lines, I told myself that there would be another actor playing a dead

Rob, and that I surely was not in control of my own destiny either. There were important lines I had to speak, but I had forgotten them. I was staring at the doctor's green scrubs, which were somehow soothing until I cast my eyes down at the small strip of cloth where the cuffs met his black sneakers. There was a thin strip of fresh blood visible there, and I wondered if it was Rob's.

The doors opened, and his face lit up when he saw one of the porters walking toward him, laughing at something someone was telling him on his cell phone.

"This gentleman is going to take care of you," the doctor said, and suddenly I was walking next to the porter, who was already calling to another man down the hallway. Unlike the hallways of the main hospital, there were no bland watercolors of canals and riverbanks. Only a vending machine at the far end that hummed loudly. Two dented metal doors he pushed open. There was no warning. Rob was the most recent arrival. They'd covered him from the neck down with a blue sheet, and when I approached him, the porter touched my elbow and told me not to remove it because there was too much trauma to the body.

If it weren't for his blue eyes, still open, perfectly intact but covered with a thin layer of gray, like candle wax, I would never have recognized him. His jaw was destroyed. There were white flecks in his hair that I would later realize were bits of his own teeth. They'd done their best to sponge the blood off his face, but it still covered his neck, as thickly as if were wearing a gruesome sweater.

It was so awful I instantly got a splitting headache. The porter was kind enough to bring me two Advil and a small paper cup filled with water. Painkillers in a morgue. I swallowed them, and then I took an insistent step toward my husband, calling out his name, as if he were just playing the game again.

"Miss," the porter said when he saw what I was doing.

The other porter came running toward me, helped the first one pull me away.

"I'll see you at the wedding," I said to my husband. Then I turned to the porters and narrowed my eyes. "It's the Old Field Club. He knows how to get there."

I guess they teach them to recognize someone in severe shock, because they both nodded their heads as if this made perfect sense.

On the way out of the room, I grabbed some paper towels from a dispenser. In the glaring light of the hallway, I looked down at my blood-soaked dress, dabbing at it helplessly. And then I walked right back into the morgue, back toward the porter who was starting to wheel away my husband.

"Ma'am," he said.

"There's a wedding toast in his pocket. Please give it to me."

They gave each other a quick look, and the one standing closer to my husband nodded. I watched him reach into the pocket of Rob's shredded jacket and pull out the three pages of the toast, still damp with his blood.

"Is this it?" he said.

CRAIG

*T*he wedding photographer had hustled me and Laura out of the reception hall before the dinner began. There was a short strip of sand and some bathhouses on the creek, and she wanted to take a few photos of us frolicking as the sun began to set. Laura had wanted the photographer to take a picture of us walking down the hill, with the Old Field Club behind us, but the photographer wasn't having it. She was one of those pros who'd done this a hundred times before.

"You want to be on the beach," she said, ushering us closer to the water. "That's where they all stand. It's killer."

"I'm too tired to argue," Laura said, looking up at me. I grasped her hand. She hadn't slept well in days, but you could hardly tell through the makeup. There was just that puffiness under her eyes, and sometimes she'd sway toward me as if she were getting dizzy. She was twenty-five years old. Seven years younger than me. Her stepfather was a bloated diplomat who'd retired in Thailand and remarried. Laura was half Thai, half Chinese, and I'd met her when I was traveling through Asia. We'd exchanged innocent emails afterward, then Skype sessions, and then a fall visit to New York, most of which I remember as awkward silence, wrong word choices, jokes lost in translation.

I was holding her around her narrow waist now, the photographer lowering her camera to admonish me one more time.

"Let's kick this up to a PG rating," the woman said, raising her camera again. "This is the moment you two have been waiting for all year. Sell it!"

Laura leaned back, my arm hooked around her. The photographer's pep talk had made me feel even stiffer. I stared into my bride's eyes, and she stared back at me as if I might let her go any second. I've seen the smile I attempted, I've seen photographs of Laura looking at me more searchingly than happily. The photograph of us running, hand in hand, up the hill, is the most convincing. The photographer snapped that one a couple of moments later, and then she walked away.

Inside the hall, one hundred and twenty guests could be heard milling around over cocktails. Kerry was standing on the deck with a drink in his hand, his face already turned bright red by the alcohol.

"You look great," he said, raising his glass to us. I grasped Laura's hand, helped her up the wooden steps as she clutched at her gown. We all walked in together, and I let strangers I didn't know take me aside, give me stupid advice, remind me who they were, and then let me spin away to the next group of elderly guests staring at me. They were almost entirely from Laura's side of the family, more specifically the Linder side. I think they all hailed from Kentucky somewhere, by way of Indiana. They all had the same long gray faces, heavy hands, greasy pearl necklaces.

"Drink more," one squat gentleman said to me, tilting his bourbon and taking a sip, "and walk two miles a day. You'll live forever."

I tore myself away from the man and escaped to the dining room, mercifully empty, and stood near the door, watching a young woman adjust the menus in front of each place setting. Twelve thousand five hundred and fifty-three dollars' worth of fresh-cut flowers sat on twelve different tables and were draped over a large stone fireplace. I walked slowly toward a table near the far wall where I knew my brother and his Rebecca would soon be sitting, and I looked down at their placards. It had been Laura who had invited them, without my knowledge. I don't even know how she'd found their address, but she'd never seen me that angry. She looked at me, more frightened than I'd ever seen her, tearfully telling me she'd only invited them because I hardly had any friends and the Old Field Club had a hundred-twenty guest minimum for summer weddings. They'd already RSVP'd.

"Do you want a bump?" I heard a deep voice say behind me.

I turned and saw Jerome, an old friend I'd first met in Bangkok. I was running low on money, and he'd helped me out by hiring me to write business-school essays for rich Thai kids. Jerome had left Stanford to travel across Europe himself. As a young black man, he had come to the conclusion that Asia was a waste of his time, and even more racist than the U.S.

We gave each other a brief, tight manly hug. He gave me a long once-over and shook his head.

"I look terrible, I know," I said. I suddenly had the urge to tell him about the phone call I'd gotten from my older brother's wife.

Jerome reached into his inside pocket, took out a small vial, unscrewed the top. He scooped out a tiny hit and inhaled. Then he lifted his broad chin toward me. Broad shouldered and tall, he had a way of making me feel much smaller than him.

"No," I said. "Probably not the best idea right now."

"That's what you said when I hired you in Bangkok," he said, shoving the vial back in his pocket and taking a long, unsatisfied look around the room.

"You really did hook me up," I said, following his gaze toward the steaming prime rib, lying under two glowing heat lamps.

"I need to ask you a favor," he said.

I knew what he was going to ask me for, so I decided to cut him short.

"As long as it doesn't have anything to do with money," I said.

Jerome's gaze had returned full circle to me again, and I could tell that he displeased.

"I think you owe me one, Mr. Krider," he said, spreading his arms out as if he'd created the whole ceremony out of thin air.

■

He was always looking for the angle on things, just as he had the first time we'd met; within the hour he'd convinced me that Myanmar was a waste of time and that there were rich Thai kids whose parents would pay upward of thirty thousand for ghost-written business school essays. Laura had been one of the first clients I'd met, and then ripped off. Thirty thousand dollars later, and despite my best efforts to impersonate her voice, she'd only been waitlisted at Georgetown.

"Wasn't for me," Jerome said, "I guess you wouldn't be standing here."

"I still think her father is going to ask for that thirty K back."

"No, man, you're in his vein now. You just keep the needle in there. I can size anybody up, and he's sitting on a mountain of cash."

With Jerome, there was always a good angle, a quicker way to get where you wanted to go.

"You want me to make a toast?" he said.

"I hate toasts," I said, fumbling around in my pocket for the few lines I'd written thanking Laura's stepfather and mother. There was a single welcome line I had to say in Thai that I was still having trouble with. *Kob kon krub.* Or was it *Krug kon rub*?

"So where's your family? Let me introduce myself."

"They're around," I lied. The truth was that my mother was the only family member who had showed up so far. She looked blowsy and fat, kept promising me that her new boyfriend was on the way, as if I cared. I could see her now, in the Lagoon Room, sitting on a bar chair, smiling at me.

"And how about big bro, where's he? Taking up a sniper position?"

"I don't know," I said, and there was an icy feeling right between my heart and stomach. Maybe some drunken night I'd told Jerome too much about Rob. I was sure I'd never told him what had happened with Rebecca. So why was I on the verge of a panic attack?

Rob's not dead, I told myself.

They're fucking with you.

Their places at table nine will remain empty all night. Trust your own instincts here. The bigger question, I guess I should've been asking my stupid self, was why I thought the game would've stopped, just for my precious little wedding?

"Hey," Jerome said, squeezing my arm as I stared up at him speechless, my mouth going dry. "You sure you don't want a bump?"

REBECCA

*S*ometimes I picked up my phone and talked to my late husband. Sometimes it was like he was sitting right beside me.

I miss things I didn't think I'd even miss about him. Even his temper. The way he could just give someone a certain look and they'd adjust their behavior. He had a way of smiling that let them know he wasn't smiling at all. By not answering a simple question, just dropping a few seconds of silence into a conversation, that would make the listener uncomfortable. He learned all those tricks from his father. Every other weekend, Rob and Craig were pitted against each other, their father teaching them how to find the other's soft spots, physical and mental.

When they were kids, Rob just sixteen, he told me he used to assure Craig he really loved him, how soon the weekend would be over and that they would be back home with their mom. But the weekends seemed to stretch on for weeks. Misery takes its time. Eventually, though, Rob stopped reassuring his brother that things were going be okay and just listened to him weep like a baby in the bunk below his.

I think of the many cruel things that he did to his younger brother, perhaps that was the cruelest of all, though there was a reason for it: Rob realized his father was listening to them. Even at night. It was nothing but self-preservation.

The boys were his father's only project. Furious that he had been left by the one human being he had ever felt a shred of affection for, their father had a brilliant idea about how he'd pay her back. He'd weaponize them. Not against the world at large, because what fun would that be for a man who never left his property in Pennsylvania? But against each other.

Rob told me the game began when Craig tried to kill him as he sat in a tree stand waiting for a deer to appear. Rob had made the mistake of falling asleep, still holding the gun.

"Tell me the story again," I said into my dead phone one night just a month after Rob had been killed. The television was on, but muted.

"You know the story," I could hear my husband say.

I wondered how long it would take until I forgot exactly what he sounded like.

"I was sitting in the tree stand by myself. Craig was in the other one with my father. Then *crack*. I remembered being startled awake by the bark beneath me exploding as the round hit it. Craig looked ashamed, and then he looked scared shitless. I must have covered the distance between the two stands in ten seconds. Broke my ankle too, when I landed on the ground. Didn't even register the pain. That's how angry I was. I would've killed him right then if he didn't look so fucking pathetic."

"Tell me what your father said again?"

"Why?"

"Because it's so sick."

"Now we're having fun," Rob said. "Looked down at me with those hollowed-out eyes."

"I've got to say goodbye," I said into the phone. I hadn't drawn the shades. My neighbor was pacing around his sparkling new home, and every now and then I knew he might be stealing a glance at me, wondering why it took me forever to turn the lights on. I just wanted to be left alone. The last thing I was going to do was knock on every door in Scarsdale and inform them of what happened to my husband.

"Craig didn't stop crying that night," Rob said. "Just calling my name again and again. Like a fucking baby. Just wanted to be forgiven, that was all. But that's the first golden rule of payback. You keep quiet. You take your time."

"Say good night," I said. "You first."

"Goodbye, beautiful," he said.

■

After I filed the police report, I asked one of the cops at the Smithtown station if they could give me a ride. I guess the guy thought he'd be taking me to the train station, because he looked surprised when I told him I was late for a wedding, and then I gave him the address of the Old Field Club and climbed in the back seat.

"No handles on the doors back there," he said. "Hope you're not claustrophobic."

I shook my head, tried to smile. I could tell he knew I was in shock, but if I wanted to go to a wedding five hours after my husband had been killed, that was my business. Anyone in law enforcement knows that people react to grief in different ways.

I was hiding the blood that had dried on my skirt with a silk shawl. Already I could see the stain starting to seep through. It was a little after seven p.m., and there was still plenty of light outside. Summer weddings.

It would be too easy to say the day had been surreal. Let's just say the only thing connecting me to the earth at that moment was the fury I felt. And the crumpled toast that I had taken from my deceased husband's pocket.

"It's a nice setup," the cop said, glancing up at the rearview. "They do a lot of weddings there. Very classy."

He glanced up at the mirror a couple more times, waiting for me to respond, but I was reading the toast, memorizing it. *I don't know where to begin. I guess I could tell you the story of two brothers who were the worst of enemies.*

What if Craig had nothing to do with it? Wasn't that possible? The first rule was no mortal injury, and they had always obeyed the rules to a fault.

The police, I told myself, would get to the bottom of who had slashed the tire. I was already racking my brain, trying to remember if there was anyone I had cut off on the road, any driver who had given me a second look, or tailgated me. Had we pissed off somebody in the next room the night before when we had sex, and had he taken it out on our car in the morning? Was the desk clerk a secret psycho? I recalled he smiled too much when I was asking him for directions to the wedding.

We were passing marshland now. I could see water through the cattails and manicured lawns on the other side. A man paddleboarding across the creek. Looking to my left, I stared down at the seat, knowing I would see my husband there, but I didn't. I think reality is so much more of a sketchy affair than dreams. It's what the world shoves on you, but it should be the other way around.

Maybe that's why I closed my eyes for a moment. I could feel him holding my hand, I really could. It's just the way he would've held my hand on the way up to the wedding, the other on the steering wheel. His thumb rhythmically moving over the back of my hand. He would be thinking about what had happened at our own wedding, and then he would pull his hand away, clench his jaw, and probably wonder why he was going through with any of this.

"Working on a toast?" the cop said, his eyes darting upward in the rearview mirror.

"No," I said. "It's finished."

"My advice," he said. "Keep it simple. Don't try to be funny. That was my mistake."

"I'm going to break their hearts," I said softly.

"Those are the best ones, honey," he said. He gave me another look in the mirror, but then I could see his expression changing. Maybe there was something wrong with my reaction, or he'd seen the blood on the paper I was reading. But he no longer felt any need to be chatty. Now he just wanted to drop me off and get back to the station.

We had turned onto the gravel driveway leading to the club, cars parked in neat rows on the grass. It was just as nice as it had seemed on the website. The weather was perfect. Swatches of deep blue water visible through the reeds. Even from here, I could hear the pleasant murmur of the guests in the dining room. The sound of silverware scraping against plates, an occasional piercing laugh rising above the other conversations.

I waited for him to open the door, and then I thanked him and slowly walked over to the white trellis near the creek. There were still some rose petals scattered on the stone walkway. Flowers tied to each of the posts, as if some harmless sacrifice had just taken place there. I sat down on one of the long white benches, scraping a bit of dried blood off the hem of my dress with my fingernail.

Then I took Rob's toast out of the pocket of my jacket again and read his words one last time. It just wouldn't do.

I would have to come up with it on the spot. It would have to be perfect. Because the best toasts are always seared into your brain. You never get them out of your head.

CRAIG

*I*t was Kerry who told me he had seen her. He said a taxi had dropped her off.

I was sitting at the bridal table, polishing off my third glass of wine. I hadn't eaten a thing. I was trying to follow the mind-numbingly tedious story of how her father had ended up in Thailand when Kerry nudged me and softly whispered that Rebecca had arrived.

"Where is she?" I said.

"She's just sitting outside," he said. "By the trellis."

Before I could even get up and intercept her, she was walking into the dining room. A waiter was guiding her to table nine. The two table settings were still in place, two empty chairs. She sat down, exchanged a word or two with her neighbors, leaned her chin on her fist, and just stared at me.

"Rebecca's here!" Laura said, leaning backward in her chair and touching my arm. Her father was still talking about Bangkok as if I had never left the conversation.

"Glad she made it," I said, forcing a smile at my new wife. Our first crisis, I told myself, would be subtly handled. All would be well.

Kerry was clinking his wineglass.

"What are you doing?" I said.

"Getting this over with," Kerry said, standing up, jerking the ends of his jacket down, but it just sprang back up on his barrel chest.

I watched her closely through all the toasts. I was able to clap, and smile, and look mildly embarrassed at all the appropriate moments.

Kerry recalled the first time I'd told him about Laura, and the atmosphere in the room became appropriately somber. This was true love. He could hear it in my voice.

Laura's father stood up and surprisingly found himself speechless. He began to weep, and the guests cooed appreciatively.

My mother stood up, looked down at me with such unexpected affection that I instantly got a lump in my throat, and told everyone that finding happiness was a waste of time, but loving someone was the only thing worth living for.

"I love you," Mom said, raising her glass, her hand beginning to tremble a little. "And your brother. And both of your lovely wives."

Laura was smiling up at her as if a saint had just given her some blessing. But Rebecca hadn't moved. The expression on her face hadn't changed. It was the look of someone who has brought terrible news but has no hysterical reason to share it. She was completely self-possessed, and heads were turning her way long before she stood up.

"Where's Rob?" my mother shouted at me from the end of the table.

"I don't know," I said, watching someone at Rebecca's table clink a glass for our attention. She was still staring right at me. She had been the whole time. An older lady at her table was looking in amazement at a dark stain on Rebecca's dress, turning to the guest next to her and whispering something as my brother's wife stood up.

"I'm Rebecca Krider," Rebecca said. "My husband, Rob, is Craig's brother."

This was going to be okay, I told myself. The prick would be walking in any moment. *Vintage Krider,* I thought. I even quickly glanced behind me. You had to be aware of your perimeter, my father always said. Keep your eyes moving, and your neck on ball bearings, because no intelligent adversary just stands in front of you, for all the world to see.

But she was.

"I don't know where to begin," she said. "I guess it's no secret that Craig and Rob were a little bit competitive. . . ."

There were a few knowing laughs, a low murmur as more distant relatives were clued in.

"Like all brothers are, I suppose," she said. "But the Kriders always took things a little further."

She looked down briefly at a piece of paper in her hand, and then straight back at me.

"Craig, you can probably remember that time you two had the Roman candle fight and nearly lit half of Rolling Hills Resort on fire."

More laughter. I nodded stupidly at my father-in-law, then Kerry. Shrugged my shoulders playfully. Sure, I remembered that little incident. The sizzling yellow and green and red balls sailing through the dry forest, bits of leaves briefly catching fire. Harmless stuff, when you consider the whole repertoire.

"Or that time," Rebecca continued, actually allowing a flicker of a smile to appear on her face. "That Rob made me shave off your eyebrows when you were sleeping. I guess they needed a woman's touch. . . ."

I listened to more laughing, remembered myself waking up on the couch, staring at a kneeling Rebecca. Something off about her smile, and then her forehead furrowing with guilt. I could still remember touching the baby-soft skin where my eyebrows used to be.

"Sorry about the eyebrows, Craig," she said.

I gave her a stiff little salute, rubbed my eyebrows playfully with my forefingers. I was grateful she was so artfully picking the few moments of relatively benign sibling rivalry, and I knew then that this could be the day that everything really did change between me and my older brother.

Where was he anyway? I mean, besides being dead. This would be the moment for him to make his entrance. Maybe without eyebrows, just for comic effect.

"But sometimes," she said, slowly raising her chin and looking up at me again. "It got a little out of hand."

I stopped nodding my head. Stopped smiling. I was amazed at how fast silence seemed to grip the room again. The waiters had even stopped talking to each other.

"I'm pretty sure," she said softly, "that Craig will never forgive his brother for leaving him on Interstate 70 when he had to take a leak."

Interstate 70, I thought. I scrambled to remember it, and then it came back to me. It was one of the last weekends we had seen Dad before he killed himself, and by then Rob was old enough to drive. He hadn't wasted any time in waiting for the right moment to watch me suffer. I had stood on the side of the highway for hours, shivering to pieces because I'd left my winter coat in the backseat. Eventually I caught a ride with a long-haul trucker. But I got back to Morningside Heights and my mother's apartment at dawn. All I knew was that it was my turn, and that I'd get him back even worse.

"Craig had to hitch a ride back with a trucker," Rebecca said. "And I guess the guy made a pass at him. Don't worry, Laura. Craig swore he just let the guy squeeze his leg."

A few less laughs now. No hint of a smile on Rebecca's face.

"But you got Rob back," she said, her voice growing quieter. "And then he got you back. The two of you were always sticklers when it came to the rules. You could do anything. But you had to wait your turn."

I listened to someone clear their throat next to me, as if that sound would somehow dissuade Rebecca from continuing. It's funny how people act when they start to get uncomfortable. At the table in front of me, I watched an older lady fiddle with her purse. A man across from her knocked a piece of silverware to the floor as he reached for his wineglass.

A good thing could still happen here, I told myself. Rob could come sauntering into the hall and plant a kiss on the top of my head. Maybe we'd hug in front of everyone and show all our guests that there was no need for turns anymore. We had finally grown up. I reached behind my chair and held Laura's hand.

"Do you remember the time . . . ," Rebecca said, staring at me, "that you sneaked a cigarette with me at my wedding? It was just going to be a cigarette."

She glanced around the room, took a deep breath as if she was savoring the smell of the flowers, and continued.

"The place wasn't as nice as this. That's for sure. It was on the other side of Long Island. Everyone was dancing inside, and Craig and I just finished our cigarettes. I was drunk. And I was angry at my husband. Because he had finally promised me that he would stop playing this game. He had promised me he wouldn't take his turn. But then he did."

The older woman at the next table was lifting one long finger now, trying to get the waiter's attention, but the waiter was staring at Rebecca in amazement. There were weddings, I guess, and then there were weddings. I would've traded anything to be him at that moment, back against the wall, holding a wine bottle, wondering what this beautiful woman's problem was.

"I was so angry," she said. "And for once I didn't feel like being the voice of reason. I guess I took my turn. I always see myself doing the right thing. Just heading back inside. But the truth is that I let Craig take my hand and lead me the other way."

I let go of Laura's hand. I was holding Rebecca's in my mind, leading her past the valet at the Venetian Club as he was texting someone on his phone, his face tinted blue. Our shoes crunching over gravel. I was looking for a good place, and then I just wanted it to be any place, some place he could even see it happening. I couldn't believe she was letting it happen, and part of me wondered if it was all planned.

"He fucked me between two cars," Rebecca said. "I held my wedding dress above my hips and I was too scared to make a sound. I can still remember the sound of him slapping my ass. That was a nice touch, Craig. And then I looked behind me, and I could see that he was taking a picture with his cell phone. How would you all like to see that one?"

It was Kerry who stood up first, as if he could possibly defend me. He started tapping frantically on his wineglass. There was murmuring now, glances shot in all directions, the panic of a crowd looking for someone to put this in perspective.

"I guess that qualifies as revenge," she said. "Because Rob did things that were just as terrible. He loved getting inside his little brother's head."

"Shut up," Laura's father suddenly shouted. He tried to stand up, but his wife pulled him down.

"I wish my husband could have made it here today," she said. "Because he wanted to tell Craig how much he loved him. There's some blood on my dress, and I apologize—"

"Please stop!" Kerry shouted. "This is the day they've been waiting for."

"And I apologize," Rebecca said. "But my husband was killed by a hit-and-run driver earlier today."

There was this strange gasping sound from the audience, like spectators watching some body falling through the air. A woman actually screamed, ran from her table. Another man yelled something angrily.

"Enough," Laura's father said. "Someone make her stop."

The waiters were urgently conferring. The chef, resplendent in his Old Field Club embroidered whites, moved toward them and quickly determined a plan of action. Three of them walked toward Rebecca, grimacing, heads down.

"Craig, you murdered my husband this morning," she said. "And I'm not here to forgive you."

One of the waiters was crouched behind her, ashamed to even reach out and touch her elbow. She ripped it away from him. The chef was saying something to her, one hand splayed out on the table, begging her. I was the only one who wanted her to finish. I was as horrified as anyone, I swear, but I could've listened to her all night. My life has just been one long uncomfortable moment.

She had my heart in her hands, is the thing. I wanted to know what she was going to do with it.

"The worst is yet to come," she said, her voice quavering noticeably now. "More awful than you can ever imagine."

Now she was speaking my language. Where *was* Rob, anyway? He was running out of time to make this even more memorable.

And then she sat down. You would've thought, after ruining my wedding, that she might have left. But she remained there until everyone else had left her table, abandoning their cold lamb chops and quinoa salads and napkins and half-filled wineglasses. The waiter, the same one who had tenderly tried to remove her, now absurdly brought her the bread basket and held out a pair of tongs.

Laura was leaning forward, and at first I thought she was saying some kind of prayer to deliver us all from this, but then I realized she was crying, her whole body frozen. I kneaded her forearm like an idiot. I told her it was all just a sick joke. A Krider thing. We never knew when to stop, after all. I swore to her that Rob was lurking somewhere. The evening could still be saved, if you could call it that.

"We can't kill each other," I said to my bride out of nowhere. "It's one of the rules."

She looked at me as if I'd lost my mind. But it wouldn't be the first time I'd mention my father's rules that night, as I got drunker and drunker.

Later on, a few guests tried to make the best of it, getting smashed in the Lagoon Room. I caught one more glimpse of Rebecca before she vanished. She was talking to my friend Jerome. He was nodding his head, a little too rapidly, squeezing her hand. But she slowly turned toward me as she spoke to him softly, immediately sensing I was there.

The right thing to do would have been to march into the dining room and embrace her. But I stood there, useless and stuck, unable to close the distance between us.

"One for the books," I heard some stranger say behind me. I turned around, my arms rigid against my sides, one fist balled up tight. The least I could do was hit somebody.

He was some nobody in his early forties, with pinkish skin, an awful thin smile.

I waited until I was a foot away from him and then I swung upward, breaking his nose. I heard chairs falling over, a glass break, and then someone was pulling my hair, screaming for the police.

REBECCA

I would spend days on the couch, staring into space, the house going dark. Unanswered emails piled up. At first, my voicemail box was always full. I deleted messages after hearing a few words of a family member's voice. Or an old friend from college, barely getting a "so sorry" out before I pressed seven.

By late August, I started to realize people had moved on. Or given up trying to reach me. My mother and sister still called, but all it took to quiet them was a text that said, "I need some time." And then that's all there was. Of course I would talk to him. The refrigerator would make an unfamiliar rattling sound, and I'd mute the television.

"You there?" I'd say.

It's not easy talking to a dead husband. They can be moody, just like they were in life. Sometimes it must have sounded like I was having a one-way conversation.

"What do you want me to do?" I'd say.

"I miss you," I'd say. And then panic:

Are you there, are you there, are you there?

By October, a thin layer of dust covered the countertops. The takeout I'd crammed into garbage bags and dragged down to the basement had started to stink. A box of once-important files had been upended on the living-room rug. Half of them burned in the fireplace before I'd lost interest. Then one night my cell phone rang, and without even glancing at the number, I picked it up.

"How are you doing?" Craig said.

I was sitting in my usual corner of the couch, cross-legged, the radiator's coils ticking behind me. It gave me pleasure, for a change, to be the silent one.

"I've been trying to reach you," he said.

I could picture him, tucked away in some corner of his home, his wife unaware. I could see his pale face, his thinning curly blond hair, the way he'd be hunching over, looking at the floor or out a bedroom window, waiting for me to speak.

"Are you there?" he said.

I ended the call. That slippery little beep must have made him panic a little, because he called right back.

"Listen," he said.

I liked the way he sounded now. Rob would've loved it. Like someone trying to talk their way out of a potentially violent situation. Not on their knees yet, but holding up their hands, backing away slowly and thinking about escape routes.

"Please talk to me," he said. "You're the only one who understands this."

This was getting even better. In a day or two, he'd be unable to function. In a week, he'd be in worse shape than me. Sitting in the dayroom of an expensive mental facility.

"You've got to understand one thing," he said.

"There's nothing more to understand," I said. "Game is over. Rob's dead."

"I would never go that far," he said. "It's one of the rules. No mortal injury."

"How's Laura doing?" I said, shifting on the couch so that I could see out the picture window. I could see the couple who lived next door, walking past each other, making dinner.

"You scared the shit out of her," he whispered, as if she were listening.

"That was just the beginning. If you really want to protect her, I'd put her on the first plane back to Bangkok."

"Rebecca, you know how this works. You were part of it."

"The game's not over," I said. "It never ends."

"He was a real fucking prick," he said, his voice tightening up. His jaw must have been clenching. "And I'm glad he's gone. Do you hear me?"

I let him go on a little. His rage coughed out a few words at a time, until it sounded like he was choking himself. His poor wife must have heard him now, losing his cool.

"I'm going to kill you," he said. "If you even think about threatening her again."

I switched the phone to my other ear. There was a moment I felt truly sorry for him. It was so easy, in the end, to get under his skin. He simply had to like you a little. And if he loved you, there were all sorts of possibilities. I wondered if Craig thought he loved me.

"I'm sorry," he finally said, defeating himself, as usual. "Good night."

When he called back again, I just put the phone under the couch pillow. I could feel it vibrating as I stared at the neighbors in their kitchen. They had even lit candles on the dinner table, to make the night feel more special. I couldn't decide if that made me feel sorry for them or envious.

CRAIG

I should have called Rebecca. It would have been the right thing to do. How hard would it have been just to check in on her, make sure she wasn't counting out painkillers for the final exit?

■

But I didn't.

Not once.

She had people she could turn to, anyway. Her mother in Manhasset. A sister somewhere. And how would it have worked besides, with Laura in the next room, listening to me talk to my late brother's wife, taking a walk down that nightmare of a memory lane?

No, I just sealed it off, like that kitchen I came back to in Astoria.

I'll never forget that afternoon I walked back into my apartment and smelled the fresh paint. There was a kid, small eyes, buzz cut, ugly thin mouth. He might've been nineteen or twenty, just finishing up. He gave me a look, like I didn't even belong in my own home. Looking back, I recognize that face now, and I wish I hadn't slammed him against the wall, asked him what the fuck he thought he was doing. He shoved me, spat once on the floor, and left, but not before giving me one last look. He looked like he wanted to kill me.

After he left I wandered around my home like an unwanted guest.

A freshly painted sickly green wall had been freshly installed between the living room and kitchen. But behind it I could still hear the refrigerator humming, smell the sweet scent of something rotting. I punched holes through the drywall all night, like I was trying to find some secret tomb in my own apartment.

■

Laura and I spent two weeks in Kauai on our honeymoon. It didn't take me long to convince her that I had nothing to do with Rob's death and that Rebecca had temporarily gone insane with grief. The thing I loved most about Laura was that she'd give me a funny look if something didn't add up, and then she'd simply move on. I'm sure, if I had wanted to, I could've run Rob over right in front of her and figured out a way to explain it away.

But I would never have done that, because I'd be breaking one of the only rules. My father had made it real simple for us to understand what they were. That's why he boiled it down to three: no mortal injury. Wait your turn. The game never ends.

There were times I watched Laura and I actually felt happy for a moment. I wondered why I had the luck of meeting the only person in the world who could possibly believe anything I was saying. And then, just like my father, call it the Krider curse, I knew in my bones it wouldn't last. It felt too good to be true. It felt like another setup. One way or the other, she'd find out the filthy truth about me.

I never thought twice about delaying the honeymoon because of Rob's death. I'd already spoken to a Suffolk County detective a few days before we departed from JFK, or who knows, maybe some guy Rebecca paid off to get information from me. I realized after he'd left that I'd only taken a cursory look at his badge, and I never got his name.

He'd shown up at my office and asked me if he could ask a couple of questions. Proving that I'd been at my own wedding hadn't been much of a problem; the guest I'd assaulted at the end of the night had filed a police report. The detective was curious about why I'd lost my temper.

"At the end of the day," I said, pausing just long enough to let him know I might just get emotional. "I might have had issues with my brother. But I still fucking loved him."

Priceless, right? But strangely enough, true.

My brother would've loved Kauai. It was his kind of place. Mai tais on the terrace of the Hyatt, kalua pig and fire dancers at the luau, not a single stormy day. At times, Laura and I would get looks, because of the age difference, but that pleased me too. I didn't mind occasionally being mistaken for her father. That might sound creepy, but it wasn't at all. It made me feel even more protective and loving toward her. I guess a shrink would say I was acting out my own father issues all over again, trying to become a better version of him. Pretending that love and protection were actually possible.

I should've called Rebecca, but the more time went by, the harder it was to even think about dialing her number.

One afternoon I hiked up the Kalalau trail with Laura, and we stopped for a few hours and just sat there watching the long swells of the Pacific Ocean below, its blue so much deeper than the Atlantic. The air smelled so sweet I felt like I was in some Yankee Candle shop, breathing in scents of vanilla, then lemon. I remember Laura turning to me and asking me why I looked so happy, as if she didn't fully trust the lightness of my mood.

I wanted to tell her the precise reason: I had finally realized Rob was dead. It was such a relief that I felt guilty at first, and then I told myself it must all have happened for a reason. Or was it possible, sitting next to Laura there, watching other hikers pass us by, that I could finally blend in with the rest of the world, and just be another happy couple, climbing higher and higher into the warm blue.

One day we tore out into the ocean on one of those high-speed tour boats, the hull lifting up and slamming back down in the deep valley of another wave. They stopped a few miles off the coast, in water so deep that the captain pointed out whales breaching not too far away. One of the deckhands dove in first, vanishing underneath for what seemed like far too long. He emerged some distance away and told us that he hadn't seen any sharks but couldn't guarantee that they weren't in the vicinity.

I was the next one to dive in, breathless for a moment. I've never been in water that deep. For the first few minutes I wondered what was beneath me, pictured my pale legs spastically kicking. And then I started to relax, stopped worrying if the boat would suddenly leave me, or if that dark clot of storm clouds in the distance would drift our way. I let go, I lay on my back and floated, thousands of feet of water below me, and I knew I had nothing more to fear. My older brother and dad were both gone and I barely talked to my mother at all.

"Roll your eyes wherever you are, Rob," I thought to myself, floating.

I was finally free.

The feeling lasted for most of the afternoon. And then that old feeling of dread returned.

I'd bummed a cigarette from some tourist, and I stood on our balcony smoking it, staring down at the flickering tiki torches and the underwater lights in the pool. I'd looked down at the bar area. Underneath the thatched roof of the bar, I could see a man's shoes on the brass footrail. His face was still hidden from me, but I watched him open a wallet, pay what he owed, and then he swung the chair around and got to his feet.

It's my brother, I thought. He would leave a five on the bar, slap the wood twice with his hand. He would get off a barstool like that. His hands looked like Rob's. Large hands, the fingers clenching as if he was getting ready to throw a punch.

But when he emerged from under the thatch of the roof, I saw that it wasn't my brother at all. Just some balding tourist standing there looking at a text message on his cell phone. I was so relieved that I felt a little ashamed. I had been ready to run into our hotel room and shake Laura from her sleep, getting out of that room as fast as possible.

The moment of dry-mouthed fear had passed. I was just a happy nobody on vacation again, and my wife was peacefully sleeping.

I could see Laura lying under a thin white sheet, her shoes neatly placed at the foot of the bed.

"He's really gone," I said softly, wishing she could hear me.

■

When someone asks me what I do for a living, I always tell them I'm in property management. It's a broad term that hides a more specific fact. I specialize in property tax and water liens, buying up hundreds of them all across the state. Anyone can bid on a foreclosed property, but the days of flipping a home for a hundred thousand dollars in profit are over. The real estate market has tightened up, so I narrowed my focus.

Say you owned a tidy little home somewhere near Buffalo, New York, but forgot to pay your water bill for one year. No big deal. Maybe you let it slide for two years and tell yourself you'll catch up on it when you sell your home. Now it's three years later, or four even, and you're just another lucky homeowner who bought at the right time and is ready to cash in.

The problem is that I now own your water bill. I've bought it at an auction and you're going to have to pay me the interest on it before you can have it back, before you're whole again. You're going to have to spend your whole day yelling at some bureaucrat at the DOB in Niagara Square in Buffalo, but they're going to tell you the same thing. If you want title to your home, you're going to have to deal with me or, more specifically, one of my very patient assistants.

My office is on the fourth floor of a dreary-looking glass-and-brick building on Livingston Street in downtown Brooklyn. I've learned to tune out the phone conversations that take place around me from nine to five. I rarely bother to remember our employees' first names. They last six or eight months and leave. Nobody likes being called an asshole by complete strangers all day.

All you have to know about my boss is that his name is Francisco and that he wears tasseled Italian loafers. Which means he's rarely here. More often you can find him on Instagram or LinkedIn, taking photographs of his cappuccino in some Lake Como hotel room. Half the time I show up for work, I'm reassured by the buzzing fluorescence of the office, and the other half I'm worried we're going to be raided by the FBI, boxes of files hauled away by men in bad suits.

"El Chapo!" someone shouted. All three of our employees had gathered at one of the floor-to-ceiling glass windows, watching a motorcade of black Escalades and NYPD cars whelp beneath us, on their way to the courthouse two blocks away. I stand apart from them, looking downward at the open rear door of a shining black SUV. I can see someone in ballistic armor, his black boot and shin guard just visible, his gloved hand clutching an automatic weapon.

"Could be anyone," I said, twisting a blind so that I didn't have to squint my eyes into the morning sun.

"No, that's El Chapo," one of our older male employees said. For a moment, I thought his name might be Patrice. He was tapping the glass with his forefinger now, more excited than I had seen him in weeks.

"Back to work, folks," I said, lightly clapping my hands. "Your phones are ringing."

And they were. Blipping in triplets. Enraged homeowners all over New York State wanting to give these poor souls a piece of their mind.

I grabbed my jacket, closed my office doors, and headed to the elevator. Though the foreclosure list had shrunk to about eight viable properties, I never missed the Tuesday auction.

Outside, the El Chapo excitement had vanished. There was no trace of the motorcade, just furling, greasy bluish smoke from the vendors who had started preparing for lunch hour. I was walking under some scaffolding, intending to grab a cup of coffee at the Starbucks on the corner, when I passed a young homeless guy. He mumbled something to me as I walked by, nothing unusual. But I knew I hadn't imagined what he'd scrawled in green marker on his cardboard sign.

Hi, Craig, it said.

When I turned around, he was already looking down the street, nodding his head as a couple of other pedestrians moved toward him. I took a step closer to him, just near enough to see that my name was no longer there, just a neatly written plea for mercy and a dollar or two.

I admit I stood there long enough that he looked at me again. "Help me out, sir?" he said to me.

Another group of pedestrians walked toward me, taking up most of the sidewalk. I turned sideways, excused myself, then accepted it was a silly mistake. When I opened the door of the Starbucks, I almost considered walking back, giving him two dollars to turn the sign around. But I told myself that if it really bothered me, I could do it on the way out, large coffee in hand.

A few minutes later, determined to resolve it so I could move on with my day, I walked out the door and saw that he was gone.

Maybe it had all been wishful thinking.

I'd come back from Kauai feeling as if I'd gotten the perfect chance to get back on track. There was no older brother who would have one eye on me, waiting to take his turn and destroy my life.

There was only one problem. Life without a close enemy is monumentally boring. I found myself on liveleak.com at night, staring at grainy video of Brazilian hit men on motorbikes. I looked for airfares to the most dangerous places on earth. One night, needing any sort of rush at all, I bought a bag of crappy coke from a dealer on 50th Street who I had passed earnestly many times with a bag of groceries, or hand in hand with Laura.

None of it did any good. The adrenaline rush of the game blew it all away. And now the game was gone for good with my late brother. No wonder my mind was playing little tricks, pathetically imagining that my name had been written on a cardboard sign.

I was the nobody I had always wished I could be, watched by no one, and there were times I had to admit, my fucked-up heart beat a little faster when I saw someone who looked like my brother, or heard someone who sounded like him, twisting my head to see that it wasn't him.

■

That night I met Laura at the Greyhound, our favorite local pub. I was running about fifteen minutes late, and I was hunched over my cell phone texting her my exact ETA. I have a thing about punctuality. The least that's required of any human being is that they show up on time.

When I walked into the pub, Laura was sitting at the bar, talking to a bartender I hadn't seen before. He was probably in his late twenties, but I didn't like how close he was standing to her. I sat down next to her and gave her a kiss, and only then did he slink away.

"Let's get a table," I said to her.

"I already ordered," she said, giving me a funny look. There was an empty shot glass in front of her. Laura can't drink. It's one of those things involving Asian genes and a minor hyperthyroid condition. She takes a sip of wine and she suddenly can't see her own hands.

I realized she was smashed, and the smirking waiter with the Etch A Sketch fuzz of facial hair was whispering something to the manager. They both turned away from me, realizing I was staring at them, still talking to each other underneath their cupped hands, eyes glittering.

"What kind of shot was that?" I said, pointing to the empty glass. I felt more like her father than her husband, and I could feel a needle-thin trickle of sweat along my spine.

"I can't tell you," she said.

"Stop being silly," I said.

"A blow job," she said, quickly glancing at the bartender's back and then back at me again.

"That's funny," I said, looking down at the drink menu. "'Cause I don't see that here."

I looked at her for a moment, alarmed at how dilated her pupils were.

We were sitting at the end of the bar, and I couldn't wait for the fucker to come back down and take my drink order. I did what I usually do at bars; I sat up rigidly and stared expectantly. He continued to ignore me, his back still turned. He leaned on the bar and started nodding his head to something a squat blond customer was telling him.

"Craig," Laura said. She was grabbing my wrist now, staring at me blankly. I placed my hand on her back to steady her.

"Dizzy?" I said.

"I'm sorry," she said. I didn't want her to be sorry. It wasn't her fault at all.

"Hey!" I shouted at the bartender. It was strange, but I had a better view of his pale face and muddy brown hair in the large tiled mirror that ran the length of the bar. He smiled vaguely at his customer, and then took his time walking toward me, wiping down the bar with a towel as he neared me.

I thought I'd start with an indisputable fact. I told him that my wife was allergic to alcohol and that he'd ruined our date night.

"Maybe a bar's not the best place to meet then," he said, turning toward Laura and looking at her with a mix of derision and sympathy. "How you doing, hon?"

It was the *hon* that did it. When someone half your age calls your wife a pet name after getting her drunk, the next few moves are fairly standard. My dead father had taught me them long ago.

"Hey, buddy," I said, standing up, my hand still firmly placed on Laura's back. "Why don't we step outside? I've got a couple of questions for you . . . I'd love to know what was in that shot you gave her. . . ."

"Sure," he said, not fazed in the least. He polished a tiny dent in the copper bar, then looked up at me and smiled. "But why don't you be a champ and take care of your girl first? She looks like she's about to throw up."

Laura grabbed my hand, almost childishly pulling me toward her. My neck was perspiring now, stiffening, the way it always does when the only possibility left is violence. The worst part was waiting for it to happen. I was always more relieved when the actual fight began..

"Let's go, Craig," she said, looking up at me. She was reaching for her purse when it fell on the floor, her compact and keys and phone sliding across the floor. I wondered if he had even helped himself to her wallet.

"Bye, Craig," he said, casually running his fingers through his greasy mop of hair. "Come back anytime. Have a nice *trip* home."

When I watched him slowly walk back down the bar to the blond woman, now impaling the gray snot of an oyster with a tiny fork, I saw two ghosts: Rob, and my father, sitting at the same bar, looking at me in amazement.

There wasn't anything I could do except help Laura to her feet, like the gentleman I always told myself I was. *Trip,* he'd said.

I hissed at him as we passed him. This time he didn't even turn around.

Forty-eight minutes later, after putting her to bed, I drove back to the Greyhound at seventy miles an hour. I burst through the door, more than ready for the fight, a small paring knife in my jacket pocket, just in case things got really ugly.

But just like the homeless guy with the sign, he was nowhere to be seen. A bar back told me the other guy's shift had ended. Just to be sure, I stayed and had a drink at a bar, served by another bartender. I asked her if she'd seen the prick who was just mixing drinks an hour before.

"Could be one of the new guys," she said. "I wouldn't now. I showed up late."

I sipped a Jameson on the rocks and looked up at myself in the mirror, the tables emptying behind me.

■

By the time I got home, I was a little drunk. I thought Laura was fast asleep, so I walked into the study and stared at some emails from Francisco, quickly growing bored with his attempts to manage a company from six thousand miles away. And then my wife was standing in the doorway, looking at me in terror.

"Craig," she said, cupping her mouth. "How come you're so far away?"

"I'm right here," I said. "Same old Craig."

"You're so small," she said. "Can you go back to normal?"

I stood up and walked toward her. I placed my hand on her back and kissed the top of her head.

"It's going to be okay," I said. "The guy slipped you something. But it's going to wear off."

I could picture him dissolving a micro dose in her drink, nudging the bar back and grinning.

"You feel furry," she said, looking up at me with a beaming smile. It was the most delighted I'd seen her in weeks. "Like a big rabbit."

"Sure," I said, holding her tighter. "I'm a big rabbit. Whatever makes you happy."

"Oh," she said. "The room is getting wavy."

I stayed up with her for most of the night until she fell asleep. And when she did, I was too wound up to even lay my head down. I stared for a few minutes at the gravestones across from us in Green-Wood Cemetery. The dawn light leaked oranges and reds across the dry grass. The fake faded flowers lay here and there in the rows, some of them blown into the trees by the wind.

I was thinking of Rebecca. After all this time avoiding her, I'd have to come up with a credible threat that would make her think twice about pulling something like this again.

"You made a serious mistake," I said out loud, wondering if she was awake too, sitting on that couch in Westchester. Telling her dead husband all about the disturbing little ways she was beginning to wreck my life.

■

I'd been deleting the last vestiges of my brother from my life. The only place he really remained was in two emails. I signed in and clicked on them. One was from December 1, 2002, the day my father put a pistol in his mouth and blew off the back of his skull in Pennsylvania.

hey craig,
   bastard's dead. see you at the funeral.

I clicked on the box next to the email and finally deleted it after all these years. Why had that been so difficult? Then I clicked on the last remaining email from my brother and moved the cursor over the delete button.

Go ahead, I told myself. Then there would be no trace of him. I'd already gotten rid of the photographs.

But I read it once more, for old times' sake. I knew he couldn't hurt me anymore:

hey bro,

I'm back home. beautiful here today with the snow falling outside. Everythings really quiet. good day to get high and plan my next big move. construction work is a dead end.

I feel like a weight has been lifted. Do you feel that?

I think it was all him. He was a sick fuck. He really got into our heads.

I don't know if we can be real brothers, watching out for each other. But I don't want to be your enemy anymore. That's what he wanted because he was lonely and sick. We were his only army. I don't even know what all this hate was supposed to train us for.

It's snowing heavier outside. Some dad is throwing snowballs at his daughters outside and they are screaming happy. Why couldn't it be like that?

It was great meeting Priscilla at the funeral. She's awesome. You're an awesome couple. And it's great to hear you're thinking of getting engaged. Pull the trigger, bro!

I think I was happy for a moment getting drunk with the two of you in Dad's house. We should have burned it down in the morning. No one should live there.

We hung out after you went to sleep and I was telling her about Dad. About the way he fucked us up. I must have done a pretty good job of making her feel sorry for us because she looked like she wanted to cry.

I held her hand a bit. I hope you don't mind.

I was telling her about the fights we used to have in the house. I think we broke every piece of furniture throwing each other into things. Don't you remember how Dad barely moved? He just sat there and shouted out the right punches and holds. I always got you in some kind of headlock in the end. I could feel the vein beating in your neck. I looked up at him once. I was out of breath and I felt you go limp.

Anyways. Sorry for going on. I was telling Priscilla all this. I had to kiss her a bit because she looked so sad. It was just bullshit the way it started, like it was better than talking about Dad. Anything's better than talking about Dad.

I was kissing her. That's all I meant to do. But kissing wasn't enough of a distraction. I felt like I wasn't going to sleep all night in that house anyway, no matter how drunk I got.

I'm sorry if it went further. It wasn't the plan. This was supposed to be the night that turned into the morning that felt like the right direction again.

But it isn't, I guess. I did something bad again. I'm telling you the truth about it because it's the last bad thing I want to have to confess.

It was early in the morning and I had to leave. You were sleeping.

You don't have to worry about her being in love with you. She's really in love with you. I'm so jealous of that because I could see it in her eyes.

Might as well be honest now. I want this to be a new day.

I fingered her a little and she started begging me to fuck her but no way I was going to do that. I really didn't mean to, but I was getting turned on because she was getting pretty wet. I don't know, maybe part of her was turned on by the idea of fucking you over and she couldn't help herself. Maybe most of us are shitbirds down deep. For a moment, I thought how wonderful you would have felt right now if I said she didn't give in.

But she did.

I put it in, I did do that, but I wasn't even really hard at first. It was just sadness/grief/shock still. Just a bad move.

I fucked her while you were sleeping and she raised up her legs and kind of had her calves resting on my back and she had really nice skin. And she was just kind of gingerly touching my back with her calves and ankles as I started to move faster. I was thinking of how terrible it was the whole time. Wasn't even wearing a condom and lord knows I'm not dating top-notch chicks like you.

I came in her hard and she was already crying without making a sound, which means either it felt really good, better than you, because you and me and you both know you're maybe a little gay and can't satisfy a girl as pretty as that? Or maybe it was because she felt terrible about what had just happened and there was no taking it back.

I think I like seeing the expression on someone else's face when they know they fucked up.

I told her if she said anything to you I'd come back and hurt her.

I wanted to tell you personally like this.

Anyway, it's your turn. Haha.

Sincerely, Rob.

P.S. The dad is still outside with his kids. They are just lying in the snow with their parkas on. He is piling up big fluffy snow all over both of them. He's burying them and they think it's the funniest thing in the world.

All I had to do was just click once and it would all be gone. But instead I hit reply and started to type.

hey rob,

   I'm really sorry you're dead. I heard it was a mess. Jesus, that must have hurt. I don't even want to think about it. :(

   How is it there? Have you run into Dad yet? Tell him I say hi.

   Do you want me to check in on Rebecca? She thinks I killed you, big brother. Why would I do a thing like that?

   It's just shock and grief she's feeling.

   I'm going to straighten her out. She needs comfort. I know you'd want me to make sure things were all right. I know you'd want me to take care of her. Of course, if you have any problem with that, just shoot me an email and I'll back right off.

                                hugs for eternity,

                                     Craig

I hit send, aware that I felt, for the first time, the certainty that I'd come out on top as far as the game.

I closed the screen of my glowing laptop, and the room grew dark.

"Craig?" Laura groggily shouted from the other room.

"I'm here, darling," I said. "Everything's fine."

REBECCA

*J*erome was twenty minutes late, not a good sign. It pissed me off because I had barely ventured out of my home for three months. I was sitting at a table near the window at the Coach Diner in White Plains. I've always hated White Plains.

I was staring at my uneaten roasted turkey sandwich, still wearing my sunglasses because the noontime sun was blazing through the window. My hands had turned a chalky white, the nails bitten down, the polish chipped off.

And then he was striding toward me. A well-built, tall black guy, neatly dressed in a suit he'd probably bought at Marshalls. He was the kind of guy who'd probably spent an hour in the dressing room while a line of people waited outside—admiring himself in a narrow mirror, shooting his hands through his cuffs.

"I got stuck in some traffic on the Hutch," he said, sitting down.

I pushed my plate to the side, picking up my cup of coffee and taking a long, thoughtful sip.

"How old are you?" I said.

He leaned back in his chair, tried to give me a cute smile.

"How old do you think I am?" he said.

He thinks he's going to get laid, I thought. He had no idea why I'd texted him the night before. You leave things vague with a guy, their gray matter tends to short-circuit.

"Thirty-seven," I said.

He looked disappointed, and then a little peeved.

"Yeah, that's about right."

He reached for my hand, just like he had at the wedding.

"So how you are doing?" he said. He tried to say this earnestly, widening his brown eyes. There was a wetness to his eyes I didn't like.

"Tell me how you met Craig," I said.

He withdrew his hand immediately, adjusted the flimsy chair underneath him.

"I used to own a consulting business in Bangkok," he said. "I hired him."

I listened to him tell me about his lucrative business-school admissions scam, though Jerome tried to make it sound like a legitimate enterprise.

"Made a fortune," he said, "and then I got bored. Wound up in Africa. Needed to do something selfless for a change. So I wound up building a field hospital in Ghana from the ground up. Talk about a project that takes years off a man's life."

I didn't buy it for a second because Jerome had never mentioned doing something selfless the whole time I had hung out with him in Bangkok. But I let it go. I noticed he was eyeing my uneaten sandwich, the slice of melted Swiss grown stiff. It reminded me of a piece of yellow, dead skin.

"You can have it," I said, pushing the plate toward him. "I didn't touch it."

I'd known how broke he was the second I looked at his scuffed brown loafers. I figured he'd been chased back home after all his angles had failed to pan out. I figured he was living at home with his parents again. I knew he'd probably asked Craig for money. After all, if it weren't for him, Craig would've never met Laura. I was also sure that Craig had blown him off. It turned out later that all these guesses were right.

But I was about to save him from all that unnecessary humiliation. As long as he humiliated himself first.

He pulled the plate toward him, tapped the slice of whole-grain toast with his forefinger. It made a hollow sound. He lifted up half the sandwich and took a bite, looking at me the whole time. He set it back down carefully, and then wiped his mouth.

"So what about you?" he said, resentment making his voice sound gravelly. "How have you been holding up?"

He watched me take another sip of coffee. I wiped some spillage off the table, balled up the napkin, and deposited it on the saucer. And then I took off my sunglasses, clacked the plastic arms closed, and did my best to smile at him.

"I guess you could say I've been a little reclusive," I said. "But I'm getting tired of being in my own head."

"I hear you," he said.

"And you seemed like someone I could trust."

It was a lie that instantly lit up his face. Pathological liars convulse with happiness when someone tells them they can be trusted. Maybe there's a neuroscientist somewhere trying to figure out that paradox. I just go by instinct.

"Talk to me then," he said loudly, doing his best to sound like he was in charge again, although no one was listening. "I'm in between meetings. I've got a client I've got to meet in Manhattan after this."

"Back to Craig," I said. "If you don't mind?"

"Sure," Jerome said. "Good old Craig."

"What do you have against him?"

"Craig?" Jerome said. "What would I have against him?"

"You were the only one who talked to me after I gave the toast."

"Maybe I just felt sorry for you. Maybe it's called having a heart."

"If you were a real friend of his, you wouldn't have come near me."

"I thought he would help me out a little more," Jerome said. "Especially after everything I did for him in Bangkok."

I stood up and told Jerome I'd paid the bill. I only had to take one step away from the table to make him rethink the question. "All right," he said. "Sit down. I'll tell you the truth."

"Tell me the truth," I said, "and then I'll sit down."

"I had a thing for his wife. Little crush."

Jerome held out his hand and pinched his thumb and forefinger to show me it was nothing at all.

"Jerome," I said, scolding him. I sat down and cocked my head. Liars who want to tell you everything always start to gush when I tilt my head like that. "You can do better than that."

"I asked her if she wanted to go out with me," he said, looking at me without a trace of slickness now. "And the bitch said no."

"Why do you think Craig invited you to the wedding?" I said. "Just to rub it in your face?"

"Nah," Jerome said, pushing away his plate.

I let that moment sink in, just pressing my lips together and taking short breaths, as if I was trying hard not to share a secret.

"He's not that kind of guy."

"Really?" I said. "What kind of guy do you think he is?"

"Listen," Jerome said angrily. "You know him better than I do.

To be honest, half the reason I showed up was that I needed to borrow some money."

"Don't ask that scumbag for money," I said. "I can help you out."

Jerome pushed back in his chair and stood up. He was holding out his hand, waiting for me to shake it.

"Like I said. I've got some meetings."

"Jerome," I said. "You've got nowhere to be. And I don't either. So let's talk."

He smirked at me, turned around to see if anyone was looking, and then he sat back down again.

"That's a ballsy guess," he said, placing his cell phone down on the table.

"So I was right about the meetings?"

He laughed at that, raised his chin a little. It was the first time he had actually looked comfortable.

"Let's just say I'm so broke I don't even have cell service."

I picked up the dead phone, stared at my own reflection in the cracked screen, and then I handed it back to him.

I raised my hand in the air, and the waitress walked toward us.

"Eat something," I said to Jerome. "I want to hear more about how you met Craig."

CRAIG

*O*n those weekends my father used to make us go deer hunting, it got to the point we had to tell him the obvious: there wasn't anything bigger than a chipmunk in that forest. But that only made him more stubborn about the whole endeavor.

There's nothing that makes you feel as empty as being stuck in a lifeless forest in the fall in Rolling Hills Resort. A few strands of dried-up leaves were still stuck in the branches, but we had a pretty good view for at least a mile. It was just leaves covering cold ground. A stone wall someone had laid in hundreds of years ago.

The day it happened, Rob was sitting with Dad in the tree stand. I was sitting alone in mine, about forty yards away. Every now and then he'd look over in my direction, but he didn't dare to say a word. It was my father's call when we'd get to go home and eat. If he wanted us to sit there like statues all night, we had no say.

My father always seemed like he was on the verge of saying something awful or threatening, but then he'd cough or spit, or take another sip from his flask. There was only one thing he was interested in, period. And that was my mother. He had given us a camera and made us take photographs of her on the sly when we were at her apartment in Morningside Heights. He gave us a dollar or two for whoever took the best secret photo of her. He even turned that into a competition.

This was before the age of cell phones, thank god, because I'm sure he would've had us surveilling her nonstop.

Back in those days, all we had to do was hand over the color Kodak photographs. He always instructed me to have them developed semigloss because it made Mom look even sexier. The pictures I took were always from far away. Mom in the courtyard, Mom bringing groceries back from the car, Mom leaving for work in the morning, all made up. That morning, from where I sat in the deer stand, I could see him sifting through some new ones I'd given him. He was going through them again and again as if he'd find some crucial bit of evidence he'd missed, and I could tell it was making Rob nervous. Dad had turned us into his own private little stalkers, and he could have cared less how disgusting it made us feel.

He didn't know what to do with the love he still had for her. He shoved the photos into the pocket of his camo jacket, and his whole face reddened.

I don't know why I did it, but I'd dared Rob to include one photograph that I knew our father would get sick over.

Maybe Rob left it in the stack just so he'd be forced to face up to the facts. The best photograph was one of Mom and her new boyfriend, drinking beers at some picnic table. Looking fucking happy. Not outrageously joyous, not mooning over each other, but relaxed and lightly holding hands, the rest of that autumn afternoon all theirs too share. But the kicker was that our mutt

Labrador, Taz, was sitting at their feet. Mom had taken the dog with her when she left, and my father didn't seem to care one way or the other. But I guess it's different when you see you ex-wife and your dog with the new guy, one of his hands on my mom's knee and the other on Taz's head, like he owned it all for good.

Yeah, that was the biggest mistake I made, daring my brother to stick that photo in there, because I think it led to what happened. What the fuck did we think would happen? It was our stupid way of getting back at him for all those miserable weekends. We were kids, and we hadn't learned to think two, three, four steps ahead.

We heard the girl's voice before the guy's. Like all hikers coming from the Rolling Hills Resort, their voices carried on the gentlest breeze. They were talking about the things all young couples talk about, laughing about the crappy food at the hotel, or how boring the trail was, or how old everyone else was at the hotel. He was trying to scare her by pretending he'd seen a snake slither in front of him. She shrieked and ran ahead.

She had a funny way of running. She was wearing leggings and white sneakers and had borrowed a baggy sweater from her boyfriend and she had shiny blond hair that flopped around as she climbed up the hill. She was the first to see us. She actually smiled and waved, and that was when my father shot her boyfriend.

I heard the shotgun explode to my left, and I instantly flinched. My father ejected the shell and yelled something at me.

I was in shock. I was still looking at her.

"She runs," my father shouted at me. "Shoot her."

I laid the rifle on the railing and got her face in my scope. She was frightened to death, of course, but half of her still seemed like she might believe it was a joke. Her boyfriend was lying facedown in a bunch of leaves and it looked like he might be playing dead. I couldn't see any blood at all.

But when she saw my father steadily walking toward her, his knife out, she screamed again and started to run. I didn't shoot, and neither did Rob. But we did something worse. We watched him catch her.

We could see everything. We watched it all through our scopes, trembling.

He was such a gentleman he even helped her as she started to fall backward, her legs bent underneath her, one of her hands slowly sliding off his arm.

I wasn't looking through the scope anymore; I wanted him to seem as far away as possible. I wanted to believe I wasn't even there, but all the littlest things became more real. Leaves the color of dried-up blood falling to the ground here and there. The rustling sound his boots made as he walked around her body afterwards. For a moment he stood halfway between the two of them, kind of crouched, as if they would rise up again. He was the worst coward down deep, scared to death of everything.

"Get down here and help me," he finally cried out to us, his voice breaking.

We should've shot him. But we didn't say a word. We looked at each other for a second or two, wondering if either of us had the courage to do it. You don't know how many times I picture myself gunning him down, and then Rob finishing him off.

But all we did was climb down from the stands, and walk toward him. We spent the rest of the day burying them.

■

The headaches started after the wedding. Understandable, considering what had happened. Eventually they were so severe that I had to stop whatever I was doing. I'd swallow some painkillers my doctor had given me and try to breathe as slowly as possible, telling myself it was only temporary. And it was. A few weeks later, I was just fine.

One rough morning, the headache came back with a vengeance. It started some time before dawn and mercilessly continued as I took the R train to work. By midafternoon, I was sitting in a doctor's office in Manhattan, staring at an old copy of *Entertainment Weekly* and clutching my temples.

Soon enough, I realized there was a young man in his mid-twenties staring at me. Buzz cut. Thin lips. Small eyes.

When I noticed his gaze, he finally forced himself to look out the window, one hand half clenched and beating nervously on his knee. I had seen him before.

He was one of the All Action Contracting guys. The last one left when I had walked into my apartment eight years back to see that my walls had been painted a delightful shade of snot. This was the little shit I'd thrown up against the wall. He just looked older and uglier now, but his nasty expression hadn't changed at all.

It was a strange coincidence, to say the least—or more likely, Rebecca had given him a little extra money to torture me.

"Hey," I said to him. "You remember me?"

He looked at me for a moment, smiled, and then he had the nerve to slowly shake his head.

I snorted out a disgusted sigh and bit my lip, trying to read the magazine again, but I couldn't get through a single sentence. When I looked up again, he was walking to the elevator, stabbing the button with his finger, pulling the hood of his sweatshirt over his head. I tossed the magazine on the table and stood up. I was walking toward him when the receptionist called my name.

"Yeah," I said, watching him step into the elevator. "That's me."

■

A few minutes later I was walking backward on my heels in the neurologist's office. I touched my nose with my eyes closed. I gripped his hands like a child and pulled his fingers back toward me as hard as I could. He shone a penlight in my eye. Hit my knee with a reflex hammer.

"Your reflexes are normal," he said. "But I'm going to send you upstairs for an MRI."

I instantly regretted telling him how much pain I'd been in a few hours before. But I did as I was told, numbly walking from one office to another. Changing into a papery blue gown in the dressing room, I heard the receptionist laughing about something and thought I heard her say my last name. I tried to reach Francisco, but there was no cell service. I thought for sure he would have left me some urgent midday messages from Dubai or Nairobi or Monaco or wherever he'd flitted to now. I shoved my clothers in a locker with a missing hinge that couldn't be secured.

When they finally tucked me into the machine, I was in an even worse mood. There was a small mirror to relieve claustrophobia, and I stared up at it. Behind glass, I could see the technician, but just barely, because he was sitting behind tinted glass. He was upside down, but it was reassuring to look at him, although everyone was starting to look vaguely familiar.

"We're going to start now," he said, his voice crackling through the tube. "If you need to talk to me, I'm right here."

The banging commenced, high-pitched, then low-pitched, the last industrial band on earth playing in an empty loft. The monotony of it almost relaxed me until I looked up at the mirror again and saw that the technician was gone.

I'm not one to panic, but the din inside the machine was becoming unbearable. The industrial band I'd been picturing to keep myself calm had packed up their instruments and left town. These sounds were different, more ominous, an intense clanking that suddenly paused, as if it were waiting for me to protest.

"Hey, how much longer?" I said.

My voice was lost as the metallic echoes smashed all over me again. I was sweating now; the foam earpiece had fallen out of my ear. But at least the technician was back, dutifully looking at one monitor and then another. Even though his face was hard to see behind the thick glass, there was something about his gestures that I recognized.

"How are we doing?" he said with vague contempt in the short silence that followed.

"I'm good," I lied.

"Okay, champ," he said. "Just a few more minutes."

Champ. The bartender had used that word. I looked into the small panic mirror in front of my eyes. Even upside down, head down, with a more clean-cut look, he could've been that prick's identical brother.

The sounds started to modulate, spreading themselves out until I was sure I could hear a human voice in it. *Brother, brother, brother, brother,* the machine seemed to say. Faster, and higher, then so low it made my heart vibrate.

"Hey," I shouted. "Is it normally this loud? I feel like something's wrong."

This time he didn't answer. He just stared at me in a bemused kind of way, and then turned toward the doorway, as if someone was asking him an important question. When it was over, and I was slowly ejected from the machine, I was ready to have a word with him. See him up close. But another technician had taken his place, a woman with her hair pulled back tightly in a bun.

"Where's the other guy?" I said. "The one who was in the control room?"

"Sorry?" she said, as if she had no idea what I was talking about.

In the changing room afterward, I sat on a tiny bench, too worn out to look at my reflection in the mirror. I dressed slowly, going through my wallet to make sure it hadn't been touched, powering on my cell phone. By the time I walked out of the building, the daylight was already fading.

■

I walked into the lobby of my office building as everyone was walking out, turned on the lamps in an empty office. There were hours of work to do. A bulk purchase of tax liens in Schenectady hadn't been purchased by the auction deadline, and Francisco would be furious.

I'm going to be late, I texted Laura, adding a tear-squirting emoticon. I was standing in front of the window and looking down at the scaffolding below. I could see the homeless guy's shoes and legs, but not the rest of him. It was the same person I had seen before. He was sitting cross-legged, writing something in black marker on a new sign. I couldn't make it out from there, but I told myself that it was probably the standard broke-and-hungry plea. Maybe a vet.

"You need some sleep," I said out loud. "You're working yourself up over nothing."

And that was true. The headache had been knocked down again. The MRI would turn out to be a complete waste of time. My new wife had just texted me back an *I love you* and on top of that a very earnest *How was your day?*

There were no emails from Francisco, just a handful from our lawyer, and then one from my dead brother. I nearly scrolled right past it. But there it was. In bold. Unread. He'd even flagged it urgent. The subject line said:

Your head

I clicked on it. Read the first four words he'd written to me from beyond the grave.

How'd it go?

I knew it had to be Rebecca, screwing with me. I was wondering how she might have known about the doctor, and then I remembered the kid in the waiting room. It was possible, wasn't it, that she would have someone spy on me?

I could picture her staring at me from across the dining room at the wedding, giving her toast in a steady voice, telling me the worst was yet to come.

I hit reply, and then I typed the words I'd been waiting to say for so long:

Hey,
    We need to talk. When can I see you?

I hovered the cursor arrow over the send button, and then I backspaced over all the words, making the page whole and white again.

I really need to

Backspace again.

I can't stop thinking about you.

I left those six words up on the screen, the cursor blinking steadily. It was true, and seeing it on the screen made it even more true. There were times, having dinner with my wife, listening to her prattle on about some software glitch, that I would've been happy to have been sitting across from Rebecca, even if she was still mad at me after all these years. I wanted to see her because she was the only one I could talk to about the game and how it was still eating me alive. But she must have known that already.

I'd been calling her just to hear her voice, and when she just stayed on the phone, refusing to say a word, it was still better than nothing.

But I was happily married, I told myself. I really loved Laura. How lucky I was to have found someone as kind and uncomplicated as her. This need for drama was just some unhealthy reflex, or twisted guilt, or just simple self-destructiveness.

I touched my forefinger lightly on the delete button and pressed down, sucking away each letter, one at a time.

I can't stop thinking about you.
I can't stop thinking abou
I can't sto
I can't
I

REBECCA

*J*erome knew I had him figured out. You don't have to say much to get under the skin of a talker. All you have to do is laugh at the most ridiculous parts of their story, and they get the message. I was sitting in the passenger seat as he drove and he was telling me something about Stanford, and how he'd decided to blow off a scholarship for adventures in Asia.

I'd given him the address of the house in western Pennsylvania, but Siri was cutting out half the time. We'd gotten lost for an hour, riding around Newark. I told him I'd pay him five hundred in cash every day to drive me wherever I wanted. The plan was to tease him into more of the dicier stuff. But I knew that wouldn't be a problem. I was a widow just getting myself back together. I needed someone to help me out.

"Anyway," Jerome said. "My grad buddies are looking at me like I'm crazy. We're sitting at a bar in Palo Alto called the Old Pro," Jerome said. "Crappy food, cheap pitchers of beer. And a mechanical bull. You ever ride one of those?"

"Yeah, I have," I said, smiling at him.

"I never got near the thing," he said. "I was getting a degree in sports medicine. I knew better."

"You can use the HOV lane," Jerome said.

"Got it," he said, merging onto it. "You just relax and enjoy the ride."

"Where did you really go to school?" I said.

"I just told you," he said. "Why would I lie?"

He was doing eighty now, already on the bumper of an SUV ahead of me. I could see the shadow of the driver lifting his middle finger toward his rearview mirror.

"Because rich kids in Bangkok aren't going to hire some guy who never went to college."

I could see him thinking about doubling down right then, but the thing about sticking to your story is knowing who you're up against. In Thailand, lying must have been a cinch. Maybe they saw a black guy in neatly pressed slacks and a blue dress shirt, and they were too intimidated to even ask a follow-up question. He could've told them he was CIA.

"How about we try this?" he said. "I'm going to tell you something I've never told anyone before."

The touching part is that he thought I really wanted to hear the sad truth. I nodded my head as he told me about growing up adopted in Chicago. Something about Harper High School. His mom dying of a staph infection after recovering from heart surgery. His janitorial job at the Harold Washington Library. A certificate in underwater arc welding that turned out to be useless. No wonder he had invented Stanford.

"Jerome," I said. I dusted a little speck of something off my knee. "I like you going to Stanford. Let's keep that story."

I could tell that a part of him, a big part of him, wanted to slap me right then, or at least tell me he wasn't going to chauffeur me all the way to Pennsylvania. But all that followed was resentful silence. His whole story was stuck in his throat, and now he had to swallow it back down, piece by piece.

"You know what?" he said.

The shadows of the bare trees we were passing were whipping across our bodies now, like nets catching nothing.

"What, Jerome?"

I closed my eyes, leaning back against the headrest.

"You've got a killer smile," he said.

I let him see me smile for an instant, but as soon as he faced forward again, I let it go. He was that easy.

CRAIG

I'm a Krider, so premeditated acts of vengeance, simmering animosity, calculated revenge—all are second nature to me.

Bump into me hard on the subway, and I'm at a loss. I need time to get angry.

It was the guy from the waiting room. Rebecca's All Action employee. Suddenly standing right next to me, pretending nothing had happened.

Some papers I had been trying to read standing up on the way to work fanned out on the dirty floor. First things first. I crouched down, picked them up. I'd barely slept the night before and was more than a little irritated.

I saw that there was one more piece of paper I'd overlooked and bent back down, but he stepped on it as I reached for it.

Funny thing about New Yorkers. All those fellow commuters, they always have one eye on you as soon as the faintest disrespect starts to happen. That's the gas this city burns on. Getting through your day without being humiliated.

It was too early to take a stand. Page thirty-seven of the Schenectady abstract could stay where it was, right under his black Adidas sneaker. I rose to my feet again and was starting to turn away from him when he whispered in my ear.

"That's right, bitch."

It wasn't particularly original, although several other passengers heard it too. I smiled at my own reflection in the window. I stuffed the remaining papers inside the prim little leather satchel Laura had bought me for my birthday, and was relieved to see that he had lost interest.

There were only three more stops, and even if my skin was getting warmer and my body had started to tremble slightly, the way it always does when I feel I'm in danger, I told myself that I would never see him again. But I'd already bumped into him twice, so I knew that wasn't likely now. Maybe it was just beginning in earnest now, the way she'd promised when she made the toast.

At Jay Street-MetroTech, he followed me off the train, not so close behind that he was stepping on my heels, but almost.

He shoved me near the turnstiles.

"What are you smiling at, faggot?" he said.

Page out of my dead brother's playbook. Because I was always painfully smiling. I could trade a few insults with him or my father, but then something in me seized up, and all I had was the rigor mortis of a grin, a Western movie set, all edifice. My face would just freeze, and I'd imagine running away. Not being a Krider. Not being me. I dreamed of a machine that would erase my mind, absolve me from responsibility. I wanted to wake up in a town, in a house, a room, a bed, that wasn't my own, and be clean . . . but it could never happen.

So I shoved him back, that was all, just like I had three years before. I knew it was a bad mistake the second I touched him. He'd wanted to kill me.

He stumbled backward a little too easily, which should've been the tip-off. I'd been in enough fights with Rob to know when I'm being lured in. He had something in his hand, and then I felt it scrape against my face. The pain leaped up my cheek a second later.

Blood was invented to be an embarrassment. Sure, it pumps into your brain and keeps you alive, but it also gets everywhere. It always makes me want to apologize at first.

I'd spun away from him now. I was holding my cheek, feeling the sting where he'd slashed me. The blood was snaking through my fingers, circling my wrist, and when I took my hand away it started pit-pattering all over my blue dress shirt, like isolated drops of rain before the storm really blows in. Then it started welling up behind my hand and fell faster. A thin, glistening trail of it followed me as I followed him through the turnstiles. I was holding out my cell phone now with my other hand, smearing the face of it with blood too, trying to take a picture of him.

I got one of him walking up the exit stairs, his profile a little fuzzy but still plain to see, both hands hooked around the straps of his nylon book bag as if he were just a student again. An older Hispanic woman was tugging at my elbow, shouting something at me. I would've chased him, I should've chased him, but it's about the humiliation sometimes. I wondered how I'd look in the bright sunlight, streaked with my own useless fluid.

"Come," the woman said, leading me toward a wooden bench like a child. "Sit down here. I'm calling an ambulance."

■

Francisco was waiting for me when I finally got to the office, wearing some fresh skin glue on my cheek that the paramedic had promised me would work just as well as stitches. My shirt was still covered with dried blood.

"I thought you were in Dubai?" I said, stepping into his office.

"What the fuck happened to you?" he said.

"Some psychopath on the subway," I began.

"This is not your lucky day," he said, slowly shaking his head.

I could never really stand Francisco. He was one of those fine-boned Euros who always seemed to show up with a year-round tan. Fond of starched shirts with thick blue stripes, he never spent more than a few minutes in this office. There were no framed photographs on his desk, no degrees on the wall; there wasn't even a phone on his desk. It was bare except for a flowery box of Kleenex. He pinched one out now, blew his nose, and then threw the tissue on the floor.

"There was an issue with the Schenectady auction," I said.

"The vendor called me this morning. That's why I'm here."

"It won't happen again," I promised him.

"That's a million-dollar mistake," he said evenly. "They won't let us rebid."

I wanted desperately to change out of my bloody shirt. That day, that week, it had all gone terribly wrong. The important thing was not to let a note of panic creep into my voice. I was thinking of the right way to tell him that he owed me one when he gently raised his hand and shook his head, stopping me.

"There's a bigger problem," he said. "Do you remember an employee named Sarah Powers?"

"No," I said. "I can't even tell you half our new hires' names. They barely make it three months—"

"She's filing a sexual harassment suit against us. She says you rubbed your groin against her ass."

Francisco tossed a manila folder onto his desk.

"That's a lie," I said. And it was. I scoured a thousand fluorescent office memories, a thousand bland interactions, trying to remember her face. I'd kept my distance from every single employee we'd ever had. I preferred to express my frustration to them through emails, even if they were sitting five feet away.

"Her lawyer served us this morning. It's pretty detailed."

I flexed my jaw, still trying to keep calm. I was aware that a fresh string of warm blood had oozed through the liquid stitch. I touched it with the back of my hand and looked at the gleaming streak on my knuckles.

"Are you going to fire me?" I said.

Francisco plucked another tissue from the box. For a moment, I thought he was going to hand it to me, but he wiped his nose again.

"How's married life?" he said, standing up.

He had the audacity to smile at me. Then he shook my hand, looking at me earnestly.

"Francisco," I said.

"I'm sorry," he said softly, pulling his hand away.

"It never happened."

He walked to the door and turned.

"There's a fresh shirt in my desk drawer," he said. "I wish you the best."

I watched him saunter away, resisting the childlike urge to call Laura and tell her what had happened. It would only frighten her, make her feel as if we were one step away from financial ruin. Instead, I unbuttoned my bloody shirt, threw it in the trash basket, and ripped the dry cleaners' shroud of plastic off Francisco's shirt. I left the office for the last time without saying one goodbye, looking just like him in thick blue stripes and stiff collar.

REBECCA

*N*othing ever happened between me and Jerome, though I'm sure he always thought I'd warm up to him. I just needed help with the little things. I hadn't slept. Sometimes, just steps away from our home, I felt a surge of panic. Couldn't go through with an ordinary task. Talking to a neighbor. Mailing a bill.

Jerome didn't complain about being my chauffeur. He knew he was getting paid, and I think he was intrigued. But as soon as we crossed into Pennsylvania, he got a whole lot quieter.

Rob's ashes were in the trunk. He'd left no instructions whether he wanted to be buried or cremated. No will. I didn't want the ashes in our home anymore. They were interfering with the conversations I had with him at night. Those long one-way conversations, waiting for his voice to break through the silence.

When we pulled up to the house, I carried them out. It was just a thick cardboard box. Inside it, the plastic bag.

I wondered why the brothers had never sold the house. I knew their father had left it in his will to both of them, but it had just been sitting there, caving in a little more every year. The shingles on one side had started to peel off. As I approached it, a flock of starlings sprayed out of a hole near the attic, coming to rest in a nearby tree, cocking their heads and wondering, I'm sure, how long I would stay. Someone had cut the screen around the door, punched in a pane of glass. They were nice enough to close it on the way out, having surely found nothing.

"Smells like shit in here," Jerome said.

I put the cremains down on the kitchen table. Heavier than I would've imagined. I'd made an appointment with a real estate agent, but this being western Pennsylvania, on a Saturday, he was hours late showing up, and when he did, he gave me and Jerome the once-over, as if we were a couple.

"Problem with this," the real estate agent said, his mop of white hair tinged with a fading sunlight, "is that buyers like to look at a little water. Any size lake will do."

"Must be one somewhere around here," I said.

"About five miles away," he said. "But it's private. And then you have the Rolling Hills Resort situation."

I asked him to elaborate. Jerome had walked out of the house. He was leaning against the car, smoking a cigarette.

"It's abandoned," he said. "Went out of business in 2009. County is trying to scrape together the money to have it torn down because it's an eyesore. Buyers see it on the drive down here, and they think this whole area is a dead end."

"Just find a buyer for this place. We need to get rid of it."

"Well," he said, staring at the box on the kitchen table. "I wish it was that easy. What's in the box?"

"Just some memories," I said.

He stepped toward me, shook my hand, and told me he'd do his best.

"The other thing," he said, "is that every local knows what happened here. Makes it even harder."

He hesitated for a moment, sucked in his lips, as if I knew exactly what he was hinting at.

"You just have to find a nice buyer who's not from around here, I guess," I said. I walked toward the door, opened it. He thanked me again but took the hint and didn't say much after that. I was squinting into the setting sun. It was unusually warm, and everything smelled like sweet, rotting foliage. It wasn't the worst place in the world. There's nothing wrong with a place on a little hill, stiff yellow leaves falling here and there, as far as you could see. A stone fence, meticulously laid out, separating nothing.

Jerome watched the agent get into his car and drive away. Then he turned to me.

"You ready to go?" he said, a little petulantly, I thought. "Because I'm starving."

"Yeah," I said, staring into the forest, wondering where they were buried. Rob had only told me the story once, cautioning me that I should listen well because he wasn't going to go through it again.

Their father had killed a young couple on October 17, 1992. The boy's name was Richard Hauser and the girl's was Monica Lansburgh. He was twenty-four and she was twenty-two. Rob and Craig were staying at their mother's house in Yonkers when it happened.

The day after, their father had called the police himself, and told them where they could find the bodies. He shot himself in the head on his front step, just a few moments after the first state trooper pulled up in his driveway.

"Rebecca?" Jerome said. "What are you looking at?"

"Nothing," I said.

I was looking down at the concrete front step of the house, as if I'd still be able to make out a bloodstain.

■

Two days later, the two brothers had buried their father at Allegheny Cemetery. There was no prayer. Just a long moment of silence, or temporary relief. Rob told me it was the closest he had ever felt to his brother. But he slept with Craig's girlfriend that night after his brother had fallen asleep. Rob told me it was because he was in shock. And when I said I didn't believe him, he told me that I would never understand. Rob wanted me to believe it was all because he'd gotten drunk and spent the last night in his father's house. Of course his father had found a way back into his blood and muscle and brain and screwed up everything.

It would always be his place, after all.

Jerome had walked back to the car and was sitting sullenly in the driver's seat, staring at me through the window. I walked toward him, head down, minding the strewn rocks that lay underneath the thin sheet of damp leaves.

"You're a smart guy," I said, standing in front of him, arms crossed. "Can I bounce an idea off you?"

"No," he said, "I think I'm good."

Poor Jerome, he never knew what was coming his way. I should have just let him drive me back to the city and let him walk away.

"You haven't even heard it," I said, smiling at him.

"What's on your mind?" he said patiently.

"Would you mind paying Laura Krider a visit on my behalf?"

"No thanks," he said. "I've got some other offers. Matter of fact, a guy just called me now."

I cocked my head, smiled at him.

"Jerome," I said softly. "Are you really going to let me down? I'm a woman in need."

He didn't say anything for a moment. He just stared through the window at the forest, a bolt of late afternoon sunlight turning a patch of dirt bright white.

"Nothing violent."

I opened the passenger door and got in, turned toward him and stared as if there was really something to admire about him.

"Don't be silly," I said. "I just want you to get under her skin a little. That's all."

"Why do you need my help getting under anyone's skin? You seem to do that just fine on your own."

"I thought you liked adventure. Trying on new hats."

He shakes his head and then says sure, placing one hand on my knee and leaning toward me. "I'll play along."

I gently circled his thick wrist with my fingers and removed his hand from my leg. He got the message and gripped the steering wheel with both hands, clenching it so tightly I could see the veins on the backs of his hands pop out.

"No offense," I said to him. "But I'm still in mourning."

CRAIG

For a few hours, I just sat on my sofa in Brooklyn, tracing the brand-new scar on my cheek with my forefinger. No matter what the paramedic said, I knew that it was going to be permanent. I was thinking of how I should explain it to Laura without alarming her, and had settled on telling her it was some random psycho when my cell phone rang. It turned out that this particular miserable Tuesday wasn't done with me yet. There was another interesting bit of news I received later that day. The neurologist called me in, and I made my way into the city.

"The glioma is the size of a pea," the doctor said, pointing to the hazy image of my right parietal lobe and a small white dot that floated there. "But we don't know if it's malignant or benign."

Then he flipped a switch, and the MRI image of my brain went mercifully dark. He turned to face me, all beard and rimless glasses. He looked more like a professor of Renaissance literature than a doctor.

I was still wearing Francisco's striped shirt. I would've happily traded places with an asshole like Francisco right then. I wondered why some men, like me, were doomed to look at a tumor the size of a spitball, and some were already on their way back to Dubai, with all the good luck in the world to spare.

"How do we find out?" I said, touching the liquid stitch on my cheek, my fingers dancing along the lazy C of the scab. Maybe the fucker had been trying to give me another hint. It was the first letter of my name, after all.

"Well, it's going to sound more scary than it really is. But we have to do a craniotomy."

He let that sink in, with a little too much relish, I thought. He told me that the position of the tumor made it impossible to perform the surgery with general anesthesia. My head would be clamped down. I would be given an injection to freeze my scalp. And then they would begin the drilling. He assured me that I wouldn't feel any pain, but I would be aware of the entire procedure, and that this was essential to prevent brain damage.

"And if I do nothing?"

"That's not an option," he said. "You could have a life-threatening seizure at any second. You're incredibly lucky that we caught this when we did."

He stood up, finished with me, a firm decision made, and warmly shook my hand. He closed his office door as I stepped into the hallway. I stood there for a moment because I thought it would probably be wise to ask him a few more thorough questions before he drilled a hole into my head.

And then I heard it: this bubbly, lighthearted giggling, as if someone was deliciously tickling him. He must have had his hand in front of his mouth, trying to contain himself, but he couldn't.

He snorted out a sharper laugh, and then I heard his fat hand slam down on his paperwork, not once but twice.

"Poor sonofabitch," he said, the mirth of it all caught in his throat now. I could imagine his wet eyes, the glasses ripped off his face, held aside as he tried to calm himself.

I should've opened the door. I should've told him I was right there listening. But the headache was coming back, sharply and mercilessly. Not just a needle or two of pain starting at the base of the skull. It was spreading everywhere, as if someone had injected acid into the space between my skull and brain.

The nurse asked me if I was all right and all I could do was nod, weakly raise an arm. I pushed open an exit door and took a seat on the fire stairs, gripping the railing with one hand. With the other, I found my cell phone and dialed Laura.

"Hey, baby," I said. And the word felt right for once. I loved her so much, because she was the only one who was going to save me. *How was your day?* she always texted me, if I was late coming home. Now I was going to tell her. And we'd find a way out of it together.

"Hey, stud," I heard Jerome Williams say. "Nice crib you've got here."

"Where's my wife?" I said.

"She's right here, Craig. Don't get worked up. I just thought I'd drop by."

I ran down the stairs, phone still gripped in my hand, and kicked open the exit door. On the corner of 57th and Fifth, I pressed it to my ear again, surprised to hear him laughing softly on the other end. I had the strange sensation that I was falling, even though I was surrounded by rush-hour pedestrians on the sidewalk. For a moment, they all seemed to have the same stern expression, their lips pressed into tight little lines, and I knew it was all a game now. Rob had hired all of them. And they all knew who I was, and what part they had to play to terrify me.

"I'll loan you the money," I said to Jerome.

"I don't need a loan," he said, all the fake humor gone. "It's too late for that."

"Jerome," I said, but he had already hung up. I watched the faces all around me, waiting for them to turn toward me, or for one person to come running toward me with a weapon, or some piece of paper to be forced into my hand with something cryptic written on it, just so the game could go on. But one by one they all stepped off the curb, and I followed them, hurrying toward the subway stairs.

■

I didn't want Laura involved. She was never going to be part of the game like Rebecca was. She would have run for the hills if she had known anything about it.

I'd met her though Jerome, and I'd met him through sheer dumb luck.

I found myself back at a bar in Patpong, drinking SangSom whiskey with another American one night, chasing it with cheap bottles of beer. He was a clean-cut guy, the sleeves of his blue dress shirt neatly rolled up. I was a little chatty, I guess. I'd been robbed in an alley near Nana Plaza, and I was still shaken up. Maybe they'd picked me out of the crowd because I looked like an uptight tourist, with my shirt neatly buttoned all the way up to my neck. A few of the buttons had popped off as I'd tried to get away, and they'd cut a neat line in my slacks, the blade just stinging me enough so that I'd offered up my wallet without any more protest.

After he introduced himself, he proceeded to give me an hour's worth of free advice. He was one of those guys who was always happy to lecture anyone, even if he didn't know anything about the subject. I think he went on for about an hour about how to avoid looking like a tourist. And then he told me about a sweet gig he'd found in Bangkok. It turned out that there were thousands of lazy little brats all across Asia willing to pay top dollar for any American who could string their silly thoughts into a coherent business school admissions essay. It was more lucrative than drug smuggling. His latest student was just a little prettier than the rest.

His tutoring sessions with Laura always took place in the airy courtyard of her parents' mansion, just east of Bangkok in Thonglor. He hated the way her mother, who looked just like an older, more cynical version of her daughter, sat on the balcony above them.

Farang dam, a servant would say to her, meaning "black guy." A fucking servant. They wouldn't leave her alone with him for a moment, and it really started to get to him. It was just another racist city.

He took it out on Laura Suttong, though. He always told me that she was one of those girls who you could tell right off the bat had zero self-esteem. He made her cry once, right in front of him, to pay her back for the servants who were whispering behind his back. Her mother watched them in amazement from above, the page of a newspaper frozen in her hand. He said that Laura delicately lowered her chin, and the tears started falling. Of course, he was never asked back, but he pretended not to care. He told me there were plenty more just like her, but I wondered if he'd liked her a bit too, and just couldn't admit that part to me, especially after he'd been sent packing.

Eventually the subject turned to life back home. After three or four rounds, I told myself if there was one person I could share my story with, it would be a stranger I would never see again.

"I needed to reset," I said. "Family situation."

"You murder some relative?" he said.

"Close," I said, laughing.

When he pressed me, I told him the truth, or at least part of it. I said that my father had committed suicide.

If I were rich, or acted stuck-up, I don't think Jerome would've taken me under his wing. The only reason he kept on buying me drinks was because he knew he was just like me. He was running away from something too.

"What's that word they keep on using?" I asked him, turning toward two young girls who had noticed the ostentatious tip Jerome had left on the bar.

"*Farang*," he said. "Just means you're white. You add a *dam* to it, you got me."

He raised his glass, touched mine.

"Here's to racism," he said. "And fucked-up families."

By the end of the night, he told me he'd hook me up with some tutoring. After all, Laura needed a new one. I guess he figured I would owe him, whenever or wherever we met again.

But when he finally asked me for money after my fiasco of a wedding, I demurred. Then I stopped taking his calls.

But I would never have met Laura Suttong if it weren't for him.

A few days after I'd met Jerome, I was sitting across from Laura in the courtyard of that mansion. But since I was just *farang*, her mother never watched over us after the first session. And pale white, buttoned-up, sensitive-eyed me, with my tight rug of blond curly hair, never made Laura Suttong feel that she wasn't innately special, that's for sure.

I lingered for hours. I heard how evil Jerome had been. And when she started to cry, I reached over and squeezed her forearm, and her tears fell on my hand. It seemed to comfort her. They always seem to think I'm a good guy. But with Laura, I actually wanted to be a good guy. Still, protecting her from Jerome was one thing. Protecting her from Rob was hard to get my mind around. She would be the first person he'd go after when it was his turn again.

The next time I saw Jerome, I bought a round of drinks. I could tell he was in a bad mood, close to hitting someone.

"You should fuck her," he said.

"Are you kidding?" I said, smiling at him like an idiot. "I'm going to marry her."

"She's twelve years younger than you."

"Eleven."

"So what's your opinion?" he said, leering at me. "You think she has fake tits?"

I stared at the bartender and grimaced as if someone was telling me a vile little story I preferred not hear.

"Lot of these rich bitches around here get their tits done," he said, "especially in Thonglor. Parents get them whatever their heart desires. New teeth. Cheekbone reduction. Breast implants. She's going to need everything they can throw at her, because she sure doesn't have much upstairs."

I was holding a bottle of Singha in my right hand, and I had to resist the urge to break it over his left temple. I could see the brown glass shattering, the blood sluicing up into his eyeballs. But this was nothing, I knew. In a few months I'd have to return to New York, and Rob would be waiting. And if I had stayed in Bangkok, he would have reached me there. He'd already sent a postcard to my address there. A picture of the Manhattan skyline and Lady Liberty, and on the back a couple of neatly written sentences:

Miss you, little bro. Don't forget to take your turn!

Jerome was still talking, trying to get any reaction out of me. Eventually he could see it was a lost cause. I was lost in something bigger. I was thinking of a question, posed in a voice that seemed foreign to me: *What if you didn't take your turn? What if you made Rob wait forever?*

"Who the fuck cares anyway?" Jerome said, tapping his bottle to the one I was still gripping in my hand. "Best of luck to both of you. But you owe me."

REBECCA

*T*he first time I left Rob, I parked my car at a gas station in Katonah and just let myself sob. It was three years ago, mid-May, I think. The game, by then, had escalated to such a degree that I was almost relieved that they religiously obeyed their late father's three commands: no mortal injury. Wait your turn. The game never ends.

But the long periods between turns almost allowed me to believe my relationship was normal at times. What I'm saying is that, even if we were in love, I knew we had a serious problem. But I was also comforted that other couples in our suburb were hiding substance abuse, secret romances, mental illness, troubled kids. And just like other couples, the periods of normalcy with Rob were so comforting that I did a strange thing: I allowed myself absolute amnesia, as if the rivalry with Craig had been some tall tale from the past, separated from us by the days, the months, and once even a year that was taken between rightful turns.

There was one night that makes me feel ill every time it passes through my mind. I'm alone in our home in Westchester, and there's a knock on the door, and for a few seconds my heart is in my throat until I realize it's just the exterminator. He walks into a kitchen filled with heavenly smells. It was sea scallops with some sort of carrot sauce that had mostly ended up on the floor. I'd had to fend off our German shepherd, Lottie, while I mopped it up.

I was making a second batch, so I barely noticed the exterminator, pumping his can along the baseboard of the kitchen cabinet. I can hardly remember his face, except to say that he was wearing your run-of-the-mill blue uniform, with his name surely stitched on his breast, and I remember the little wheezing sound he made as I opened the door for him and that he was perspiring a little. The only odd thing, really, was that on the way out, he wished me a lovely night. It was the word *lovely* that stuck in my head long after Lottie drank from her poisoned bowl of water. She had started to pant at first, and then went into convulsions, her legs kicking back even as she lay on her side on the gleaming kitchen floor. I did my best to help her, sitting cross-legged besides her, weeping as I listened to Rob's voice on my cell phone, telling me that everything was going to be okay.

He knew what had happened immediately. He knew who it was. He even said all the right things for two or three days afterwards. But when we scattered our dog's ashes on the Hudson River, near a park where we had spent most of a year together as a seemingly healthy unit, it was Rob who turned to me with a smile, waiting for me to meet his eyes.

"I can't wait," he said, touching my hand. "How about you?"

For a moment, I had no idea what he was talking about. A vacation we'd actually been planning? Or maybe just getting back to the house, away from the floating ashes of our only pet? Then I knew he meant his turn, and that, worse, he thought that I was just as excited to get revenge. Maybe he even thought I'd been mulling over the delicious possibilities.

I didn't reply. I didn't say a word on the drive home. I think we might have watched some television, headed to bed early. I lay awake most of the night as Rob slept, wondering how he could just sleep. His brother had hired a man to invade our house and kill our dog, yet Rob had passed out within minutes. The sound of his even breathing made me furious.

The worst part was that Lottie's dog bed was still sitting in a corner of our bedroom, the pillow creased where she'd slept on it. A chewed-up rotten rope toy lay on the floor beside it. It seemed surreal to me that someone could have conceived something this cruel and gone through with it, but it made me even more sick that my husband would soon think of something that would be even more twisted. It was like living with an addict who had relapsed. The year of living normally had evaporated, just like that.

It was the next morning, after he had left for the city, that I packed a few days' worth of clothes and drove away. He kept calling me all the way to Manhasset, where my mother still lived. The missed calls added up, nearly a hundred of them by the time my mom opened the door of her home and held her arms wide open.

"Best decision I ever made," I said, hugging her.

The next day, I drove to Brooklyn. I walked right into Craig's office building. I felt a little nauseous in the elevator, unsure of what I would do when I saw his face.

He was surprised to see me, I could tell. But he hid it quickly with one of his pained smiles. There were some employees milling around us, half smiling and eyeing us. He led me down a short hallway to a dark office, turned on the lights.

"This is the boss's," he said. "He's never here."

He closed the door behind us and then sat nervously on the edge of the desk. I took a step toward him, just so I was close enough to hit him. I still didn't know what I was going to do.

"You poisoned our dog," I said. It was crucial to me, at that moment, that I made him understand exactly what holding a dying animal you loved was like.

"I don't know what you're talking about," he said. He was looking at a spot on the floor, avoiding eye contact.

"She suffered," I said. My voice was catching in my throat. Just speaking about her brought it all back, her black nails scratching on the linoleum. The white foam from her mouth clinging to my jeans. The feeling of wetness as it soaked through.

He had taken out his phone now. I thought he was going to call the police, but he started swiping his forefinger across the screen. I slapped it out of his hand and pushed him backward.

It was fucking magical for a second. I took another step toward him and pushed him hard again. If there had been something sharp anywhere in that office, I would have picked it up. There was nothing, though, just a box of useless tissues on the edge of the desk.

Craig started to lower himself to one knee. *Is he going to beg me now?* I thought. *Blow his brains out, just like his father, with a handgun in the drawer?*

But all he was doing was reaching for the phone again, which had slipped under the desk. He picked it up and rose to his feet again.

"I want you to see something," he said. He handed me the phone, but I refused to take it. Raising it to my eyes, he forced me to look at the image. *Just some girl,* I thought, dark complexioned, turning toward the camera and smiling as she sat at the table at some restaurant. He swiped to the next photograph. Another woman, lying on a hospital bed. Her face swollen and eyes shut. Intubated.

"Who are they?" I said.

"Same girl," he said. "Just someone I liked. Her throat was so swollen they had to do a tracheotomy."

"What happened?"

"Oh, it was beautiful," he said bitterly. "You know when the waiter comes to your table and asks you if you have any food allergies?"

"Is she okay?"

"Yeah," he said, slipping his phone into his pocket and looking at me hatefully. "She's okay."

"Rob wouldn't do that."

"He wouldn't?"

He stood up and opened the door.

"I wouldn't either," he said.

There was only one thing I could say that would make me remotely feel better.

"It's Rob's turn," I said softly. "And two minds are better than one. This is going to be the best one ever. It's going to fuck you up so badly, you're going to want to kill yourself."

"I want to kill myself all the time," he said, looking right at me.

I told him he was pathetic. That seemed to have an odd effect on him. His eyes practically lit up. I realized I'd made a huge mistake. He'd misinterpreted my disgust as an opportunity. That's all that anyone had ever shown him. What else did he have to go on?

"Come on," he said. "Why don't we go get a drink or something?"

"It's ten in the morning, asshole," I said.

"Shit," he said, looking at his watch. "I wish I were as smooth as Rob. I'm sorry."

I heard myself ask him if that was all he was sorry about. When he opened his mouth again, I thought he'd finally tell me he felt awful about the dog.

"I'm sorry I can't say one fucking thing that would make you like me. Because I don't think you have any idea how much that matters to me."

I walked away, but he shouted one more thing at me.

"You dirtied your hands a long time ago, Rebecca. You can't have it both ways."

■

He was right about that, but I still didn't let him buy me a drink. One word he'd uttered had the intended effect. *Smooth*. After four months, I returned to Scarsdale, but I came back a little more coldhearted, trying to imagine what it must have been like to be on a date with Craig one moment and then breathing through your neck in a hospital bed the next.

The worst part was that I had been the one who gave Rob the idea for that one. Smooth as he was, he just never let me know how it all panned out.

I guess you could say I still loved Rob, or could convince myself on the good days that I still did. But there were some nights I just pretended I was on his side.

Craig had actually come up with the one word that made me start to vaguely like him.

Smooth.

CRAIG

*T*he subway ride back to Brooklyn was excruciatingly slow. I was so anxious about what might be happening to Laura that I realized I was cursing out loud each time it stopped, staring at my worried face in the window.

When I finally emerged in Brooklyn, at the 25th Street stop, I knew I was being followed again. Not by the kid who'd slashed me in the morning, but by a young woman wearing a faded red hoodie. I turned around once and she stopped too, snapping some chewing gum under her tongue and pretending to look at her phone. I continued walking up the stairs, pushing through the turnstiles, checking my dead phone. The woman followed me all the way to 28th Street and then just stood there, watching me walk up my block. I turned once more, memorizing her bland blond curls, pale face, texting someone while she bit her lip.

Jerome Williams was not making himself at home on my sofa, or making himself a sandwich on my kitchen island. I had braced myself for that possibility, but it turned out he was long gone. And so was Laura.

I called Jerome, got his chipper-sounding voicemail.

"Call me back now," I said, my throat getting tight. "Or I'm going to find you and kill you."

I was throwing a bag on the bed, mindlessly stuffing it with clothes, a razor, socks, a sweater, determined that I would be leaving there as soon as I had some idea of where they were. My cell phone was ringing.

"Everything's fine," Laura said, her voice barely louder than a whisper. "Just do what they say, okay?"

"Laura . . . ," I said. But there was nothing I could really say. How could I let her know that she wasn't protected by the rules of the game? I'd have to admit that I'd been lying from the moment I met her, and that I knew her life was at risk all along.

"He's saying I have to go," she said.

"This is all going to turn out okay," I lied. "I promise."

I heard a rustling sound. A brief cry of protest. The phone was being taken from her.

"I love you too, man," Jerome said. "This is some sick shit you have going on. Why didn't you tell me about this back in Bangkok?"

"You have to bring her back," I said.

"Talk to the boss," he said. "You know who that is, right?"

■

I didn't wait for Rebecca to call. I dialed a car service and was dropped off outside 14 Elm Street in Scarsdale an hour later. I had the whole ride up to think about Laura. It made me sick to think of how terrified she must be. The driver flicked his eyes up at the rearview as I dry-heaved once, then powered down the window to get a blast of cold air.

Laura was the only person I'd ever tried to protect in my life. The rest of the world could have gone up in flames, and everyone in it, my own self included.

But there was a question nagging at me as we sped past the gray waters of the Hudson, the Palisades on the other side a disheartening brown like shoveled earth: what if I didn't even know what I had been up to? What if she had been bait? Subconscious bait, but bait all the same. What if I had simply been working out a move before it was even my turn? Just like our father taught us. Was it possible I had brought her back to lure my older brother to the wedding? He would've been too curious to refuse the invitation. He would've wanted to see her in person, and see exactly what my heart was up to.

All those years my brother and I had been at each other's throats, and I'd never made this journey once. But I pictured him living in a house like this. Two roofs. A porch. A sloping lawn. Three tall pine trees looming over everything. There was a FOR SALE sign near the curb, the agent's name, and then PENDING.

I stood there for a moment on the curb, staring at the white colonial on the hill.

I was watching his neighbor rake leaves. He was wearing a blue parka vest and faded old blue jeans, and he shielded his eyes against the sun to look up at me. I think for a moment he must have thought I was Rob, because I saw him start to wave, and then he stopped.

REBECCA

I saw the car pull up and I stood by the window for a while, just watching him. If Craig had been dressed in a cheaper suit, he might have passed for some real estate agent, slipping his business card in doorjambs.

"He's here," I yelled up at Rob.

Craig was staring to his left, and I was suddenly worried he'd arranged to have someone meet him there. Or maybe someone sitting in a car down the road who'd keep an eye on him, make sure he didn't vanish forever inside our happy little home.

It was our neighbor, I realized, who'd caught his eye. I turned and saw him standing frozen over his rake, snug and warm in his sweater and thick corduroys, one step ahead of the holidays as usual. I watched our neighbor start to wave at Craig, probably mistaking him for Rob, who hadn't been seen in months.

I heard footsteps above me. Slow, purposeful. The floorboards creaking under his weight. He'd gotten heavier.

"Camera's working," I heard Rob say. "Just make sure he doesn't look over at the bookshelf."

I didn't answer him. The neighbor had gone back to raking his neat pile again, keeping one wary eye on Craig as he made his way up to the house.

CRAIG

I saw a hand part a white curtain, and I knew whoever was inside had seen me. I walked up to the front porch, wiped my shoes on the doormat, and pounded on the door. I didn't say a word when Rebecca let me in. I waited for her to close the door, and double lock it as if there was someone really dangerous out there she was worried about.

"You've never been here," she said softly. She crossed her arms. The wool sweater a size too large for her. I realized it was Rob's. Swore I could even detect his smell.

"Where's my wife?" I said.

"She's fine," she said, walking toward the kitchen. I realized the home was completely empty. The floors polished. Every utensil put away. The furniture gone. We stood facing each other at a corner of the marble island.

"I'm going to call the police," I said softly.

Rebecca was unimpressed. I thought she looked exhausted, but somehow she seemed to look even more beautiful tired.

"What happened to your face?" she said, starting to reach out toward my cheek as if she might touch it.

"One of your people slashed me," I said. "How many do you have working for you?"

"I don't know what you're talking about."

"Remember the toast?" I said. "You told everyone what was going to happen."

The light was suddenly strange inside, a cloud perhaps, drifting over. The whole place smelled like wax, all the windows closed. I wondered if there was still a bed upstairs. Where was she sleeping?

"You murdered my husband, Craig," she said. She cocked her head and smiled at me just enough to let me know I would never be forgiven. "You killed your own brother."

"Rebecca . . . ," I said, lightly tapping the counter with my fingers. There were so many ways to begin this speech. I had worked it all out on the ride up there. I wanted her to look into my eyes, that was the important thing. But my eyes were staring to get moist. I wiped away a tear with a knuckle, then dabbed at the other eye.

"Oh, this is good," she said, turning away from me.

"I admit Rob and I hated each other. You know how much we did."

The word *hate* made her look at me again. It was the only word, I realized, that I could really work with.

"It wasn't even your turn," she said. "Don't you know the rules? You can do anything you want. But you have to wait for your fucking turn."

She hit me then. Caught me flush on the temple and cheek with her open hand. I started to bleed from underneath the callus of the liquid stitch again. I could feel the bony outline of my eye socket throbbing, where she'd made contact with her wedding ring.

I had to move toward her. Cut off any means of escape. Then I'd pull her down and strangle her right on the floor of her empty home. But I couldn't move an inch.

I watched her reach out to me again, her hand hidden by the long, lumpy sleeve of my brother's sweater. In a million years, he would never have touched my cheek like this, blotting away fresh blood.

"I'm sorry," Rebecca said, and she looked like she truly was. "There isn't even a paper napkin left here."

"You can hit me again," I said, my stupid eyelids welling up again. "You can hit me all day if it makes you feel better."

I took a step toward her and she let me hold her, my cheek brushing against her hair. I could feel how stiff she was, but she didn't push me away. I kissed her neck once, testing her, but she still didn't protest, so I kissed her there again and breathed in deeply.

"Do you like the way I smell?" she said.

"I don't know," I lied.

I reached down and ran my hands along the sides of her thighs and then underneath her sweater. Her skin was warm underneath it. I thought of Laura for a moment, being driven somewhere by Jerome, that worried look she would have on her face. She'd frown at him, watching him talk about nothing at all, and then she'd wonder what I had gotten myself into.

"What's wrong?" Rebecca said.

I had taken a step back. I was just looking at her now.

"Where's Laura?"

"I'll tell you later," she said, crossing her arms and then pulling off her sweater, tossing it on the floor. "You've got to finish what you started. It's a Krider rule."

I moved toward her again and lifted her up on the kitchen island, her arms around my neck now. I unbuttoned her jeans like a teenager and tugged them all the way down to her ankles before yanking them away. I kissed the inside of her thigh and pulled her closer, my lips pressed against the crotch of her panties now, dragging them aside with my forefinger. I closed my eyes, pulled her hips closer, so that my tongue could get deeper inside. Her fingers were in my hair, grabbing it so that I could feel my scalp stinging.

I looked up once and saw her leaning back, her arms stretched out behind her.

"Do you want to fuck me?"

I didn't answer her, I just unbuckled my pants and entered her. Her eyes had gone hazy, her fingers unbuttoning my shirt so she could see me inside her. I was fucking her harder now, my hand on her throat. I should've strangled her then, choked her until her wide brown eyes rolled back in her head. I leaned forward and pressed my mouth against her ear.

"I'm glad he's dead," I said.

She moaned, I swear, and I knew part of her was nearly there. I just had to slam against her harder, kiss her ear, her neck, until she could say it too.

"Do you have any idea," I said, red-faced now, coated with sweat, my knees scraped raw by the kitchen drawers, "how much I love you?"

She did a strange thing then, and it made me feel just like the useless bastard I was, would always be. She shook her head and held one finger against her lips.

"Shhhh," she said. "The walls have ears."

She pulled away from me, reached out for my hand and helped me onto the marble island with a laugh, as if it was some kind of lifeboat and we were in the middle of nowhere. I lay down, and she got on top of me, grinding against me until she had come, her hair snaking around my face. I grabbed a fistful of it, tugged it behind her neck. I kissed her stomach, the underside of her breasts, her dark nipples. And then I lay back down again, on that cold marble, and listened to the steady wet slap of her skin against mine.

"Look at me," she said, holding my chin in her hand so I couldn't turn away when I came inside her.

She kissed me once afterwards, then hopped off the island as if it had all just been business, gathering up her clothes.

"Hey," I said. I was still sitting on the counter, self-conscious now about my nakedness. Trying my best not to look ridiculous on that cold slab.

"Hey what?" she said, pulling on her jeans, pulling down her bra, scraping a strand of her hair away from her forehead. She was looking down at her fingers, buttoning and buckling. Then she bent over and picked up that lump of a sweater and wriggled into it. She took a step toward me, giving me a wry smile, the first sign of real trouble.

"Just . . . ," I said.

"Are you going to ask me what just happened?" she said. "Try to talk it out . . . like a bitch?" She could sound so cruel, almost instantly. I wanted to explain that to her. I thought, if we were going to spend the rest of our lives together, she might want to work on a few things as well.

"Listen," I said.

"I let you fuck me again. That's it."

"He's dead," I said. "There's no need for you to feel guilty."

She picked up my pants and tossed them to me, then my balled-up shirt. She was shaking her head. Forcing a short, spiteful sigh through her nose.

"Not good at all," she said, turning away.

I heard it then, very distinctly, the creaking sound of someone walking upstairs.

"Who's here?" I asked her.

She just shrugged her shoulders.

"Nobody," she whispered. "It's just you and me. Isn't that what you wanted?"

She was smiling at me vaguely, still casually picking at something on her sleeve. Behind her, I could see the neighbor raking leaves.

"No one's here," Rebecca said as I started to walk toward the staircase. She was right behind me, but that didn't worry me until she pressed something cold against my neck, and I knew, without even looking, that it was Dad's old Ruger .44. He'd held it against my neck before, my face and chin, even between my eyes. I knew how the muzzle felt. Familiar.

"Let's go," Rebecca said, lowering the gun a little so that it sat between my shoulders. "And remember, I'll blow a hole in your back."

We walked toward the basement door, blue sky clearly visible through the picture window. A V of sparrows changing course in the distance and whipping upward. The peaceful world outside, raising its middle finger again. Kriders could go to hell.

"Garage," she said.

The rest of her instructions were all single words. *Light. Keys. Drive. Silence.*

She hit the garage door opener and the door rolled back, the sunlight pasting itself to the walls, my brother's carefully hung work tools. I backed out of the garage and took one last look at the second-floor windows of her home, but there was no one there.

Once or twice, speeding down the Jersey Turnpike, I stole a glance at her and the heavy gun cradled in her lap. I could probably have taken it from her and swerved onto the median. But then what? What if she just opened the door and walked away, maybe even right into traffic, beyond caring anymore?

There's something that's been gnawing at me a long time, and maybe no one else will understand. I liked being under her control. Those were the only moments I felt something like a sense of peace.

REBECCA

You know I sometimes talk to him," I said to Craig as he pulled onto the turnpike. "Even though he's a ghost."

After I'd pulled the gun on him, Craig hadn't spoken a word. He was aggressively quiet now, but I knew I could fix that. I just had to talk about Rob.

"If you were the neighbor, watching me," I said to him, "you'd think someone was really there. It's like I'm talking to someone next to me on the couch."

Craig was speeding by Newark Airport now, Manhattan to our left. He turned to me and said something, but his voice was cut off as one of the planes roared over us and landed. I could smell jet fuel, even through the closed window.

In the side-view mirror, I could see a long line of other planes descending, their landing lights popping on in the distance like dingy stars.

"So what's with the gun? Where are you taking me?"

"I just wanted to go for a ride," I said softly. "It's the only way I could get you to leave."

The sky was turning a deeper blue over Staten Island, and hearing another jet blast over the car, I found myself wishing I was at some gate at the airport, wishing I was on a flight to anywhere.

It was time to see Plan B through, and I didn't know if I had it in me. The first time, I'd done everything Rob had told me, right down to the last detail, right down to the blood I'd have neatly packed in a test tube. He'd carefully sliced the tip of his own finger one night months ago and watched it fill up, smiling at me the whole time.

In the restroom of the gas station in Smithtown, I broke off the seal and let it soak into the hem of my dress. No one normal would ever do that. I was one of them now. I might as well have been their long-lost sister.

From there on out, I'd have to play the part of a widow. I'd have to act as if I believed it myself, otherwise who would I ever convince?

"Well," Rob had said to me that night, "tomorrow's the big day."

"I'm not your whore," I said.

"It's got nothing to do with that," he said angrily. "It's all part of Plan B."

"Plan B is you coming back from the grave. That's good enough."

"You don't get to back out," he said, looking at me with such smug confidence that I wanted to hurt him. "This is high stakes now. Every move counts."

I stood up and walked toward the stairway. I could hear Rob behind me. Before I made it to the first step, he'd pushed me to the wall. He had his hand on my neck, just firmly enough so that I could feel the blood beating in my neck. Just enough pressure so that I could feel it in the back of my eyes.

"I'm done," I said. The words didn't come out like I wanted them to. I think he could see that it was almost like begging. He was shaking his head, even more confident now. Being his hostage would've been easier. At least I wouldn't have played along for five months, pretending he was dead.

"The game never ends," he said, softening his grip on my neck and giving me a quick kiss on my forehead, as if he were anointing me.

"Please," I said, watching him walk back into the living room, making sure that he hadn't left any trace of himself behind. He picked up a pad of paper he'd been scribbling on, an empty glass that had been filled with whiskey, and then he walked past me and climbed the stairs up to the bedroom.

"I think I'll spend the night here," he said. "I think that's a risk I can take."

He'd been holed up at his dead father's place, worried that Craig would send someone to check up on him in Scarsdale. He knew the last place in the world Craig would ever want to visit was western Pennsylvania.

I was happier when he was gone, and there were even nights I thought about calling Craig to ruin the whole plan. There were a few times I even imagined what it would be like if Rob wasn't around. Not just absent, but really dead.

I looked up the stairs and saw that he was waiting for me, and that he actually had the nerve to smile sweetly at me, as it was just another brisk, early winter night in the suburbs.

"Love you, baby," he said. "Aren't you feeling tired?"

I shook my head, even though my body did feel exhausted.

"Come on," he said "Big day tomorrow. Let's get some beauty rest."

∎

It was just after we'd crossed into Pennsylvania that I broke the silence that had built up between us. Craig must have known that I'd never have the nerve to shoot him.

"There were two toasts he had written," I told Craig. "But I swear I didn't know which one he'd choose until the morning of your wedding."

"I'm sure it wasn't a hard decision for him," Craig said softly, refusing to turn toward me as he drove.

"You're wrong," I said. "He really struggled it with it. You've got to believe me."

The memory of what it had felt like to run my hand through his tight curly hair was still vivid, his face between my legs. I always hated submissive men, so I suppose the joke was really on me. Craig had spent his life overcompensating, trying to keep up with his brother's natural aggression. Eviscerated when he found out that Rob had slept with his girlfriend the night of his father's funeral, he had plotted his revenge one solid year. The sad thing is that never once in his life was he truly able to be himself. His whole life had been one long tragic reaction. That's what I thought, but how was I going to tell another human being, on the night he would be brutally killed, that he had wasted his life?

"I don't believe anything you say," Craig said.

I had the first toast in my pocket, and I took it out. I'd kept it with me all this time because I wanted Craig to read every word his brother had scrawled on that yellow piece of notepaper. I had to believe the unread toast had always been a possibility.

"I want to read it," I said.

"You can do whatever you want," he said. "I'm your hostage."

"I don't know where to begin," I read. "I guess I could tell you the story of two brothers who were the worst of enemies. Who did things to each other that will never be forgotten . . ."

"There is one thing I can't forget," Craig said. "But unlike that garbage you're reading, it's the truth."

I was folding the toast carefully again, in two, then in four. I always wanted to preserve it. If Rob hadn't written those words, I never would've done any of this.

"Rob killed the girl's boyfriend," Craig said. "Dropped him like an animal, about a hundred yards away from the house. He's the one who started the killing."

"Your father did all the shooting," I said. "The case was closed."

"You know what a real coward is?"

"Tell me, Craig."

"He's someone like me. He sits in a tree stand and watches his father talk his brother into killing an innocent guy. And he does nothing to stop it."

"Are you finished?" I said. He looked so tortured then, as if the memory of the dead girl was more horrifying than anything his older brother could do to him.

"Rob was the first one to pull the trigger," Craig said. "I remember the kid fell without a sound. And she stood there for a moment and none of it made sense. She kept calling his name as if he'd just get up. I think she needed to believe it was just a game. Some prank her boyfriend was pulling on her, even as my dad walked toward her with the knife."

"Strange," I said, the saliva in my mouth drying up. When I swallowed, it felt like I was choking on something acidic. "Because that's not Rob's version."

"I don't care who you believe," he said. "I'm just sick of lying through my teeth. You're the only one who knows what scumbags we are. But you never run away."

"We'll see," I said.

CRAIG

We stopped once, at some rest stop on the interstate.

"You disappear," Rebecca said, "then Laura is going to get hurt."

She put the gun away as we pushed through the glassy doors into the fluorescence. In the men's room, I stood in front of the urinal, trying to process what was happening. I'd have to speak to Laura. I needed to hear that she was safe. And then I had to convince Rebecca that it wasn't in her interest to continue playing the game on her late husband's behalf.

Back in the parking lot, I almost felt dizzy as I walked toward her. She was leaning against the passenger door, and when she saw me coming, she opened it with a smile.

"So honored," I said.

"Get in," she said, the smile disappearing.

I climbed inside the car and took a deep breath. I had one or two things I'd been waiting a long time to tell her, and now was as good a time as any. I wanted to tell her that I'd always felt we were meant for each other. I wanted to tell her that I completely understood that she missed the game and that we'd find a way to replace it. She could give up my dead brother's last turn forever, because we were going to find joyous and cruel ways to amuse ourselves. Best that Laura be cut loose before she could be hurt. Craig Krider, protector of the innocent and lovely Laura, was just a part I was already sick of playing. That much was becoming clearer to me every day.

I watched Rebecca pass in front of the headlights, open the door, and climb in. The keys jangled and she started the engine. I was never going to be as smooth as my brother, but I knew this was the last chance I'd have to convince her.

"Rebecca," I said. "I've been thinking about something pretty hard."

"Hold on," she said, reaching down with her left hand and popping the trunk. "I forgot something."

I thought she was telling the truth, even as the gleaming top of the trunk popped up in the rearview, even as I heard the thud and grunt of someone stepping out. In the side-view mirror I could see my brother's hand grasp the rear door handle and pull it open. He was sitting behind me now, impossibly. I could hear the dry sound of him rubbing his hands together.

"Fucking cold back there," he said, touching the back of one of his chilly hands to my cheek. "Hey, brother."

"You're alive," I said. The back of my neck went hot, then cold. An animal again, that's all I was.

"Yeah, well," he said. "Death really didn't work out for me. Not as much fun."

I watched him take the gun from Rebecca.

"What's the plan?" she said.

"You know what the plan is," he said. "You always know what the plan is. That's why I love you."

I could feel his breath on the back of my neck. My dead brother's warm breath. Kind of incredible when you think about it.

"Your dad's place?" she said.

"Yeah, Dad's place," Rob said. "We've been through this. But wait one moment."

She looked up at the rearview mirror, at her husband's face. I wanted to see his expression too. More than that, I wanted to turn around and see that he wasn't there at all. But he was stroking my hair now with his fingers. Mockingly, of course. Bringing his lips close to my ear.

"Tell me, sweetheart," he said. "Your heart's in your throat right now. Isn't it? You feel sick to your stomach?"

He knew I wouldn't say a word. Admit that my world had been turned upside down one more time, and that this was the worst I'd ever felt. Wasn't that the dark beauty of this thing, that neither of us could say it wouldn't get worse?

"Are you ready?" Rebecca said.

White light cracked my field of vision, and I felt the pain flare before I knew he'd hit me with the gun. It was too dark in the car to even see my own blood, but I felt it sliding between my shirt and my skin. I thought he'd hit me again, and so I leaned forward as if I were preparing for a head-on crash, and I heard him laughing.

"What the fuck were you going to ask my wife?" he said. "What were you thinking pretty hard about anyway?"

His hand was on my back, rubbing it, taunting me. I felt the car reverse and I leaned back again, looked out the window as we merged with the rest of the traffic.

∎

Dad's house. I knew in my heart we would all wind up there again. It was getting dark. I couldn't see too far into the woods, and I didn't want to.

"Leave the headlights on," Rob told Rebecca. "There's no light in there."

She left them on and we got out of the car and walked toward the house. Rob was following a few feet behind me, still holding dad's old Ruger. I noticed the broken glass in the front door and pushed it open. There was blood on the floor. I could see that immediately, even in that moldy grayness. There was a pool of it already congealed on the kitchen table. The man who had slashed me on the subway was standing in front of us.

"You two have met?" Rob said.

"How's the face?" the man said, sliding his forefinger down his own cheek, to remind me. "Healing nice?"

"Leave him alone, Rustem," Rebecca said to him.

"Listen," Rustem said, turning toward Rob. "It got a little messy with the girl and the black guy. But everything's okay now."

The light in the windows had turned the deepest shade of blue. Soon we would only be illuminated by the headlights, which only caught patches of our skin and the wall, turning it an ugly white.

The word *messy* was making me feel sick. I wanted to believe that the turn he'd taken this time was nothing but playful. I needed to imagine that Laura was at a diner with Jerome, drinking coffee. Her phone in his pocket, but otherwise as safe as she'd always been. Or that Laura was waiting for me back at home, keeping her end of some bargain, but unharmed.

"Where is she?" I asked my brother.

The question sounded so helpless suddenly, and my throat started to tighten. I wanted him to tell me it was all okay. But he didn't answer.

"Rob," I said. "Please."

It was as if I was lying on the bottom bunk bed again, in that moldy room, waiting for the sound of his voice.

"She's just taking a nap upstairs," Rob said, smiling at me, but without pleasure this time. "It's been a long day."

I lunged at him, but the kid tackled me, driving me into the floor.

"I'm going to kill you," I said, craning my head up toward my brother.

There had to be a stronger word than *kill*. Kill was too light a word to use on him.

"Easy there, Craig. Just take a deep breath. You're getting all worked up."

"I'm going to fucking murder you," I shouted as Rustem swung down on me, crashing his knuckles into the base of my neck. I scrambled out from beneath him once, and almost reached my brother's leg before the kid landed on me again, bringing his forearm down on my temple, tugging my left arm up until I felt the tendons burning.

"Tie him up, sit him down," I heard Rob say. Rustem dug his hands underneath my armpit and started to lift me.

"Come on," Rustem said, letting out a high-pitched laugh. "Let's be a happy family."

■

Rob took a seat at the kitchen table, but I refused to look at him. The headlights were throwing strange shadows on the wall. Revealing things I never would've noticed in the daylight. Near an armchair, an old stack of dusty paperbacks looked like they would finally all fall over. The television, one of those rear-projection antiques my father had watched twenty years ago, looked as if it was filled with gray liquid.

Every piece of furniture in that room, even that cracked kitchen table leg, had been broken at least once. My brother and I had tumbled over everything, thrown every object at each other we could get our hands on. I'd stabbed him in the thigh with a rusted switchblade, wishing I'd done more damage as he rained his fists down on me. He'd smashed a glass over my head and stood back in horror, and then amazement, as a perfectly circular crown of blood appeared high on my forehead. The next day, Dad made us repair everything: glue shards back together, table legs, even the torn covers of old books.

Now I could feel Rob looking at me, but I preferred to take one last look at this bachelor museum. I could see the back of my father's head, staring at the television as he watched *Blood Creek* for the hundredth time. He loved the bonfire scene, where the hick spikes the jug they're all drinking from with tranquilizer and passes it around. After my mother left him, my father thoroughly enjoyed watching women in peril.

Rob put his hand on my shoulder and I moved away.

"Little brother," he said. "Why are you crying?"

He sounded like he meant it, as if he was really surprised that tears were just rolling down my cheeks.

"Fuck us," I said, wiping the fluid away, because that was all it was in the end. Just something else that got in the way.

"All four of us?" Rob said, taking the gun from Rebecca. "Or just you and me?"

I turned and looked at him then. Being in the deep freeze, or whatever safe house he'd been hiding in, hadn't done wonders for his complexion. His face looked fatter. I could see the hump of his stomach, like some actor's pillow, wedged under his flannel jacket. There were pouches under his eyes, deep creases.

"Put on a little weight there," I said, nudging him with my hand. He leaned over toward Rebecca, as if I'd pushed him harder than I did.

"Lost a little hair there on top," he said. "You think it's the stress?"

"Honestly," I said, "I don't think so. I always feel pretty relaxed after I fuck your wife."

Rustem snorted out a laugh and then looked up at Rob and realized his mistake, ironing out his expression again.

"That's a messed-up thing to say," Rustem said, glancing at his boss for approval.

"It *is* a messed-up thing to say," Rob said, turning toward Rustem now and looking at him with calm interest. I wouldn't have pissed on that kid if he was on fire, but I felt like warning him, telling him how close he was to being dusted off the face of the earth.

"I'll wait in the car," Rebecca said.

"Sit down," Rob said. "This won't take long. I'm just trying to remember . . ."

I watched him rub his face, breathe in deep, look up at the ceiling, as if he was really trying to remember something.

"I'm sure you are," I said. He snapped his chin back toward me. Nothing gave me greater pleasure than getting under his skin. I would stay there the rest of my life until it all sloughed off, until he was nothing but walking bones.

"Trying to remember how this all got started. Let's be serious now. I really want to get to the bottom of it."

"You thought I was really trying to kill you."

"Were you? Tell us the truth, Craig."

"No," I said, remembering my father whispering in my ear as I took aim, telling me to wake him up.

My leg was starting to shake again. I placed my hand on my knee, trying to steady my nerves. I felt like I was starting to lose it again. Maybe it was the way Rebecca had turned away from all of us, disgusted at everyone who sat around this old poker table. I wanted to tell her I wasn't like him. He was a natural born prick, just like our dad, and he lived in terror of only one thing—losing his wife the same way that fucker had.

"He's shaking all over, Rustem," Rob said. "You know what that means?"

"Pussy boy?" Rustem offered helpfully, staring at Rob a little too eagerly. He watched the gun in my brother's hand, watched him place it briefly on the table in front of him, roll up his sleeves, and then pick it up again.

"That's not a nice thing to say," Rob said. "He's just a little scared. You want to see a neat trick?"

Rob put his hand on the back of my neck, squeezed it gently twice. All the twitching stopped. The trembling vanished.

"Going to be okay, little brother," Rob said. "You don't know why I'm here. You don't know what I've been thinking. Remember, there's still three rules. No mortal injury. Wait your turn. No end to the game."

Rebecca turned to him then, her mouth parting. She tilted her head to one side, trying to gauge his real mood. It was like staring at some expanse of wind-whipped ocean, waiting for some dark shape to reveal itself or swim away forever, hunting for something else.

"Don't let him get your hopes up again," I said to her, remembering how lovely her voice had sounded when she had read the toast earlier, as if she wanted to believe it more than anything that was happening here.

"I'm letting it go," Rob said, taking his hand off my neck. "I was driving up here and I realized it's not too late to get this right. There's people getting machine gunned and blown up and drowned and burned alive every second in this miserable world, and I can't forgive you for fucking up my wedding?"

I looked at him, his face really screwed up, the furrows above his eyebrows visible as if he really meant it.

"It's true," Rustem said. "It's not such a big deal."

The kid, I had to hand it to him, had managed to stop Rob cold again.

"Not such a big deal," Rob said, staring at him icily. "It shouldn't be, right? Other brothers have done this to each other. And worse. So what makes me so special?"

Rebecca was holding his free hand now. He tore it away from her, and she grabbed it again.

"You fucked up my sex life, little brother. I have to admit that. It's like I start making love to her the way we always did, and suddenly I think she's looking at you. But there's ways around that, right? We could all live in one house. Maybe we even fix up this place. And you fuck her as much as you want, but Rebecca . . ."

He was looking at her helplessly now. Funny how easily she bought it.

"You just don't leave me, okay?"

She nodded her head.

"I'm not leaving you," she said.

"And fucking Rustem here," my brother said, his larynx tightened by emotion, strangled by the goodness of his own story. "He could even help around here. You up for that?"

"Yeah, sure," Rustem said emptily. I could tell he wanted nothing more than to escape, but there must have been vast amounts of money involved. My brother never got too far ahead of his employees. He knew how to keep them on a string.

"Sounds like a plan," my brother said, raising his chin a little and looking at some spot on the wall, or through it, up the hill where those young lovers had come walking toward us long ago.

I watched him stand up, then offer his hand to Rebecca like some kind of dandy.

"No," she said, giving me a frightened look and then turning back to Rob. "The game ends now."

His expression changed one more time, upset that he had disappointed her. She let him touch the top of her head, smooth her hair back as she stared at me.

"Sure, baby," he said. "Let's get out of here."

She stood up, and took a few steps ahead of him. He lingered for a moment, looking down at me.

"I'm going to miss you," he said.

■

After my brother and Rebecca had left, I shifted around in the chair, took a deep breath, and looked up at Rustem. Rob had given him the gun. A nice piece, but really old. Very heavy. I told myself it hadn't been used since my father last pulled the trigger, but something told me the gun would still work perfectly.

Rustem was on something. I remember trying to narrow it down. Speed, coke, K2? Or maybe he was a natural ADD freak. He was telling me that everyone knew he was good with his hands, and very early on they could see he was a fighter.

"Listen to me for a moment," Rustem said to me. He shone the flashlight on my face. "Tell me what you think of this idea."

He told me about a machine that makes things cold very fast.

"Like a microwave except it's the opposite," he said. "Sometimes your ice cream is melting. You want to make it solid again. Or your beer is too warm. Men would use it to save money. And if it was small enough, and I think maybe shiny, women would use it too."

I didn't say anything. I was trying to figure out how much my brother had paid him. It was important to come up with a figure just a bit higher, otherwise it wouldn't be believable.

"Another idea," he said. "Say there is something I put in your brother's car. Like a small bomb. Right under his seat. And there is an app on the phone I have right here. I press a button and he blows up."

"Show it to me," I said.

"Sorry," he said. "No bomb. But how about this? Tell me what you think."

"Shut up. Do what you have to do."

"Your wife is still alive," he told me. "Don't you want to see her again?"

"Where is she?" I said.

"You want to know?"

"Yes, please," I said. "Tell me the truth."

"Upstairs," he said. "In the father's bedroom. She just has tape on her mouth. She's doing fine."

"Laura!" I screamed.

"Shut up," Rustem said.

I made my move then. I guess he'd known it was coming. With my left arm, reaching all the way back to hit him as hard as I could. He moved his head to the side effortlessly, then grabbed me by the throat. He crushed the bridge of my nose with the side of the gun. Just like that. It couldn't have taken more than three seconds.

I was on all fours now on the floor. He was very efficient. He was reaching in the pocket of my jeans. He had my wallet now, and phone.

"There's a video I want to show you sometime," he said. "There's a guy who can knock people out without even touching them. It's all mind control. I believe one day I can do this."

He had a few zip ties in his pocket. He placed the heel of his boot on my rib cage, and then he kicked me over.

"One zip tie around the wrists," he said. "For the feet, I like to use fishing line. I unwind it from a spool like I am fishing, wrap it around their ankles very tight so that it bites into their skin."

I wanted to know what had happened to his other victims. They would all say they could do something for him. This was the moment I had to make my offer. With the zip tie tight around my wrists, I must have looked like I was praying to him.

"Your bank passwords," he said, taking a pen out of his pocket. "All of them."

He clicked it with his thumb and sat down at the kitchen table again, ready to write it all down on the back of his hand.

I tried to speak to him, but a web of blood sank back into my throat.

"Spit out the blood when it fills your mouth," he said. "Otherwise I can't hear you so well."

■

I think an hour or two had passed, though it was hard to know if any time had passed in that dank home. I was still curled up on the floor. Rustem was talking to me, nudging me with the toe of his boot to make sure I was still listening. I could hear the wind raking dead leaves against the siding of the house, and I had an image of myself on that warm day in October, twenty-four years before. The day the young couple came walking toward our field of fire.

The girl stopped talking first when she saw us. Her boyfriend had his head down, and he was standing about thirty feet behind her, still laughing about something they had been talking about. That was when she waved to us. This is what I can't forget; the tenderness and worry mixed into her expression, as if some part of her already knew what would happen. It was just a little help-less wave of her arm and a quick smile. Her hand froze in the air when the shot rang out, but she still had that pleasant expression on her face.

He would never get closer than thirty feet to her. Of all the awful things about it, sometimes it's the simple facts that haunt me the most. The heartbreaking math of it.

"Okay," I heard Rustem say. "Let's do this."

He sounded farther away now, and I realized that I was strug-gling to stay conscious. I spat another mouthful of blood on the floor and felt a surge of pain between my eyes, where he'd whipped me with the butt of my father's old gun. I heard the screen door slam, the hollow sound of something metallic being dragged up a step. The kid entered the house again and set the gas can near my head. I could hear the fuel sloshing inside.

"The boy was your age," I said.

Rustem didn't say a word. I saw him squeeze the cap of the gas can and twist it off. He poured a neat circle of gasoline on the floor around me, splashed some on my body. I could smell the sharp foulness of it, even through the drying blood in my nostrils.

When I think of the young couple walking toward us, I always make myself stop remembering it as soon as I see her face. The tiny wave. The smile that's too anxious and friendly. Their whole world, as small as it might have been, was so perfect just a minute before. When I think of them, which I often do, I wonder how long they would've been in love. Would they have gotten married or divorced? Had kids? Dog or cat? Suburbs or city? Shitty jobs or great ones? Where would they have ended up living?

I know why Rob wanted to pull the trigger, because I was just about to.

The kid looked so happy.

"Do you hear something?" Rustem said.

I didn't hear a thing, but I spat out more blood, rubbed my chin against the floor, and raised my head.

"Yeah," I said. "Like voices?"

"Be serious now," he said.

"I am," I said. "Like a boy's voice, and a girl's?"

"Yeah," he said. "Why are they laughing?"

"Sounds like some of the honeymooners from the old Rolling Hills Resort," I said, hearing voices too. "But they closed it down twenty years ago."

REBECCA

We'd stopped for the night at a motor inn in Foxburg, Pennsylvania. Rob had been working up a speech for his brother's funeral-to-be. Easier than his struggles with the toast, I guess. He scratched a few more words on a piece of paper at the desk in the motel room and looked up at the mirror. I was lying on the bed, still wearing my coat. I'd nearly fallen asleep.

"Best to just gloss over the sordid Bangkok love triangle, don't you think?"

"Where is she?" I asked. "And where's Jerome?"

"My brother's rage is still a mystery to me," he said, ignoring the question, practicing the eulogy. "I've asked myself again and again, when I can't sleep: what is it I might have done to prevent this? If I had just been closer to him, I could have gotten him the help he needed."

"Answer me," I said.

None of this had had been part of the plan. The rules were to be followed, to the end.

"Why wasn't I closer to him?" he continued, wearing his best poker face. "I could have prevented all of this."

His cell phone rang and he picked it up. I could hear Rustem's voice on the other end.

"Boss," he said. "We're all good."

I felt this unexpected tightness in my chest, imagined that Craig was really dead. Rob put the call on speaker, just so I could hear every word for myself.

"It's done?" Rob said.

"Everything's ready," Rustem said. "Ready to burn it down."

"Make sure you shoot Craig first, then the fire. I don't want to take any chances."

"I just did it."

The news instantly changed my husband's smug expression. His mouth was wide open, but he couldn't utter a word.

"Boss," Rustem said. "Are you there? I've got a little problem. Some kids running around in the old resort or something. I can hear their voices."

"You're imagining it," Rob said, trying to compose himself again. "There's no one up there."

"Yeah, maybe," he said, but I could tell he wasn't sure. "I'll take a walk up the hill. See if I see anything."

"Light it and leave," Rob said. "It's as simple as that."

"Sure," Rustem said, wavering.

"Rustem," Rob said. "Listen to me. You don't need to go walking up any hill. There's no one there. It's a deserted hotel. Do you hear me?"

"I'll call you back," he said.

He ended the call and hit redial, glaring at me. He took the page he'd been working on and looked at it for a moment. He tore it into four neat pieces and dropped them on the floor.

"I feel sick," I said.

He gave me a concerned look, because I really did look a little pale when I looked at myself in the mirror. I think he wanted to believe, even then, that it was all going to be over soon. He just had to get the kid back on the phone and get him to focus. Even if he had broken the rules, the game would finally be over.

"Take a walk," Rob said to me. "Go get some fresh air."

He reached for my hand, but I only let him hold it long enough to feel my fingers slipping away. I let the door to the room close behind me, and I stood there for a moment. I heard my husband make a funny coughing sound. It took me a few seconds to realize he was bawling like a kid.

"What did you do?" he burbled at himself between sharp breaths.

I leaned closer to the door. I had the key card in my hand, but I couldn't insert it. I heard him throw something against the wall and then the door. I flinched and backed away. He was yelling at himself again, calling out Laura's name and then asking himself what he'd done over and over.

I turned and walked down the hallway, his voice fading away. I dug into my pocket and felt for the car keys.

CRAIG

I *hose voices.* There was a moment I thought they weren't real, and then I knew they must have been some squatters from the old hotel. But I didn't have to tell Rustem that. He looked anxious for the first time, as if the place might really be cursed.

"I can hear them laughing," I said to Rustem.

"It's freaking me out," he said. "What are they doing in the dark?"

"It's the dead kids," I said, just to screw with his head. "That's the sound of their voices."

"Bullshit," Rustem said.

"He just wants to kiss her," I said. "She's playing hard to get."

"Yeah," Rustem said sarcastically, squatting beside me, carefully avoiding the reeking gasoline. "I hear it now. Just like you said."

The voices had stopped, and I let the silence sink in a bit before I turned toward Rustem again.

"You better run," I whispered.

"What did you say?" Rustem said. He slid out the tray of an old box of matches. Struck one, held it to my eye, blew it out. He picked up another.

"They're not fucking around," I said.

"Too bad you'll never get upstairs," he said. "See what I left for you."

"Run!" I shouted, my warning vibrating uselessly along the wooden floor. I closed my eyes for a moment. I wanted them to be real. After all, I really could see it all over again. The rifle shot. The boy dropping. Harmlessly, as if he were playing dead. A small cloud of gray gun smoke rises through the branches of the tree I'm perched in, past the railings of the stand, as steadily as a kid's balloon. The girl still standing there, her hand still suspended in midair. She's watching my father climb down from the stand; she's unable to move. It's as if she's waiting for him to come tell her it's all a joke. A sick little Krider prank. We'd all be in on it, even her dead boyfriend. Everything's going to be okay.

There's a small shattering sound, and I'm in my father's house again, watching Rustem run over to the kitchen counter, kneeling there with a gun as if a SWAT team had taken up positions outside.

"They're throwing rocks," he said.

"They know we're here," I said, feeling nauseous again, but thankful that some teenage squatters had come close enough to the house to torture Rustem a bit. I coughed up another dark clot of blood, spat the strings of it on the floor. I heard Rustem strike another match and toss it on the floor. A thin line of blue flame followed him as he ran out the door. I could hear his boots on the driveway, and then the fire leaped higher, making a sound like someone blowing into an open microphone. I could feel it on my shoes and legs now, burning off the fishing line.

I was running through a burning room. I was lurching through his home one more time, the whole kitchen on fire now, the flames rolling up the walls, black eyes growing larger on the ceiling, replaced by even bigger and blacker eyes. A thin carpet of gray smoke followed me up the stairs. In my father's old bedroom, I saw my wife's body on his bed. Jerome was lying next to her, his mouth open and his nostrils caked with blood. His right hand was clasped around a handgun.

I knelt next to Laura and touched her black hair, matted with blood. She was lying on her side, but her hands were zip tied, and when I pulled her toward me, her arms had already gone stiff. Downstairs, I could hear something shatter, layers of heat blanketing me. I started to slide my arms underneath her legs and neck, and then I stopped. Wouldn't it have been like me to try to carry her to safety when it was much too late?

So I left her there. I stood at the foot of what had once been my father's bed and just stared at her.

I might as well have killed her. I felt as if I had. I should have stayed in the room just to honor my agreement. I had only promised I would take care of her, from the moment I squeezed her arm in the courtyard of her home. In my mind, Laura is always lowering her head, and I don't know that she is crying at first, until I feel the water on my skin.

That's my best moment, and my worst. It was all beyond forgiveness now.

I started to cough, tears in my eyes. The smoke rose steadily, as acrid as burned plastic. I kissed her once on the cheek and thought of the most awful thing. Even at the end, she would've believed I would save her. She was still wearing her work outfit, a smart black dress and a beige sweater already ruined by the smoke coming up. She'd placed her shoes side by side on the floor, as if she would step into them again.

Outside, I heard someone shout my name. I could barely hear it through the noise of the spreading fire. Another rock shattered the bedroom window. They knew I was still there.

I backed away from the bed and stood at the top of a staircase already crawling with thin flame. I stumbled down it, fell, picked myself up again. The last few feet, I'm blind, hands stretched out in front of me, choking on the heat.

I could still kill him, at least. There was that. And that was no small thing.

I knelt on the front step for a moment, the heat from inside spreading all over my back, raking my neck. I could smell my own burning hair, glittering pieces of it falling on the front of my shirt. All I could do was wait for the kid to shoot me. I was going to die just where my father had. In the doorway of his home, the back of his head missing, his eyes open, as if he were still waiting for us to show up one last time. One more final, awful weekend we would always be trapped in.

I closed my eyes and heard the kid returning, his footsteps lighter now. I felt his hand on my wrist, wondering why he had become so tender suddenly.

"Craig," Rebecca said. "Let's go."

The important thing about Krider vengeance is that you never change your expression. I knew exactly what my brother wanted then, wherever he was. He wanted to see one last look of hope break across my face, and then the realization that none of it could be true. He wanted more than a look of defeat. He wanted to me to exhale it like a last breath.

"Where is he?" I said, unable to struggle against her pulling me up. She led me down the driveway like some haggard prisoner, my hands still bound by the melting zip tie. I mumbled the question again and again to her, turning my head to the left and right, trying to peel his face from the darkness.

REBECCA

*I*t wasn't more than twenty minutes before we were back on the interstate. I didn't know where I was driving to. I couldn't go home. I couldn't go back to the motor inn. Craig sat quietly in the passenger seat, and then he asked me where I was taking him.

"I don't know," I said. "I'll drop you off anywhere."

"Where's Rob?" he said. "Is he going to pop out of the fucking trunk?"

"I left him at a motel in Foxburg."

"I bet."

My cell phone was ringing.

"It's your husband," Craig said, scraping some dried blood off the bridge of his nose. "Aren't you going to answer it?"

I shook my head and accelerated. Craig reached for the phone and answered it.

"Hey, big brother," he said, the thrill of his escape making him sound a little strange, like when you get excited and your throat seizes up a little.

"Hey, little brother," I heard Rob say.

"I just wanted to let you know that everything's all right. I'm with Rebecca. Do you want to talk to her?"

It seemed like forever before he spoke, and when he did, he sounded so defeated it made me feel nauseous.

"Yeah," Rob said. "Put her on."

Craig pressed the phone to my ear as I drove.

"It's over," I said.

"You're right," he said. "It is."

His voice didn't sound the same. He sounded as if he'd given up, and I knew that couldn't be true.

"Where are you?" I asked him.

"I'm standing on a bridge, looking down at some shitty river I don't even know the name of. But I'm pretty sure I'm not going to float away too far. It's mostly rocks down there."

I was slowing down now. Eighty, sixty, thirty. I was pulling to the side of the road

"Tell me the truth," I said.

"Here it is," he said. "I pray to God that I might be a better person."

"I'm on my way back," I said. "Just wait for me."

"I love you so much," he said. "Put him on, okay?"

Craig took the phone from me, and I pulled back onto the highway. Foxburg was sixteen miles away. I figured I could make it there in ten minutes, and then I'd have to find the bridge my husband was standing on and the nameless river he was about to drop into.

"Are you still there?" Craig said into the phone. "Talk to me. It's my turn, Rob. You broke the rules. Do you hear me? Do you know what that means? I'm taking the game to a whole new level."

"I love you," I heard Rob say to him.

I grabbed the phone from Craig and pressed it against my ear. But there wasn't a sound on the other end, not even white noise.

"Rob," I said. "Talk to me. Are you there?"

■

I saw my husband vanish. I was speeding up Route 58 and the bridge was still about half a mile away. As soon as my headlights hit him, he was over the railing. There wasn't a sound, or a scream, or anything. He just disappeared, and I braked hard and climbed out of the car.

I was trying to get my breath, telling myself that if anyone was going to play a trick on me, it was Rob.

"You think I'm going to fall for this?" Craig said. I heard him slam the door and walk up behind me. I was leaning over the railing now, and I could see my husband's legs. He'd landed just where the scramble of rocks met the black river. I shouted his name, and then I ran back to the near side of the river and started down. I could hear Craig calling to me from the bridge.

"Got my eye on you," he shouted. "You're losing your touch."

I was level with the river now, walking as fast as I could across the stones, slipping on the filthy moss that covered them, cursing, making my way toward him. The first thing I did was pull him a foot toward shore, so that he wasn't lying in the river. Part of his face was okay, but part of it had been blown up to twice its size, as if it had been pumped full of air. He wasn't breathing. His eyes were open. His hair was soaking wet, cold to the touch.

"Wish I had a camera," Craig said, looking down at us from the bridge. "Because this is a good one."

"He's dead," I shouted up to him. "Please help me."

There was a moment I thought I could see Craig's expression change, as if he was really worried, but then he actually smiled and blew me a kiss.

It was so quiet where I was, and my husband felt so heavy. I'd turned him over so that his head was resting in my lap. Upriver I could hear some voices and see the silhouettes of people watching us. And then one of them was getting closer, a middle-aged man who was carefully making his way toward me, a flashlight in his hand, painting the river rocks white and then shining it on my face.

"Hey, miss," he said. "We called for help. You all right?"

I heard myself thank him. I was holding Rob under his armpit, as if he would be dragged away by a river that barely had any current. The good Samaritan was getting closer, and when he saw what kind of shape Rob was in, he switched off the flashlight.

"Jesus Christ," he said softly.

My husband's real death put the fake one to shame. All those details I'd thought I'd care about if he died were wrong. It was the silence now that was so terrifying. The wet rocks pinching my legs when I shifted position, that stranger patting my shoulder. Upriver, I could hear someone's cell phone ringing, some stupid ringtone quickly cut off. Farther off, some volunteer driving toward us in an ambulance, the siren pointless and wrong but comforting at the same time.

What was I going to say to Rob? I don't believe in God, but I believe in prayers. I don't know if that makes sense, but maybe none of this does.

"It's going to be all right," I said to my husband. I knew he couldn't hear me, but I knew he'd want me to say something stupid like that, and then lean over, kiss him on his wet forehead.

The stranger was still standing behind me, and I nearly opened my mouth and told him the biggest lie of my life. I was going to tell him that my husband was a good person, just to let one human being know that before he was taken away. And I believed that right then, as I held Rob close and his body sagged back toward the river.

But this is the thing about Rob Krider. Even as I held him and listened to the black water dribble by, there was a moment I thought he might move, that he would squeeze my hand and look up at me.

"Please tell me this isn't real," I gently asked him.

"I see you talking to him," Craig shouted above me. "You think I can't see that?"

I raised my head and could see Craig standing on the bridge, the headlights of my car streaming past him, smearing the railing white.

"His eyes are open, you stupid bitch!" Craig screamed. "He's looking right at you and you're talking to him."

The stranger who had come to help me kept his hand on my shoulder and looked up at Craig, who had begun to pace back and forth on the bridge.

"How much did they pay you?" Craig screamed at the man. "How much did they pay all of you?"

I listened to Craig's voice echo in the riverbed, his accusations flying toward us. He was right, Rob's eyes were open—but he was really dead. I'd known it the second I pulled him from the water. There was some black grit on his cheek, and I wiped it off with the heel of my hand and wiped away all the wetness from my own face so it didn't touch him. I was rocking back and forth, trying to find the rhythm of something underneath all of that sadness, but there was only Craig's screaming, demanding to know the names of all the actors who had been paid to stand around this suicide scene. At some point, the men he was yelling at must have started walking toward him, and I didn't hear his voice anymore. Then I heard the sharp sound of my car door shutting. He gunned the engine, and then he was gone.

CRAIG

*J*ust so you know," I said, looking up at Rebecca, and then down at the piece of paper in my hand again. "I'm only playing along.

"But, c'mon, where's the camera?" I said, leaning closer to her. "Where's the microphone?"

"There's no camera," she said. "No one's watching you right now—except for me."

"Yeah, right," I said softly, glancing outside. I wouldn't fall for it again.

We were sitting in a coffee shop near the Immaculate Heart of Mary Church in Scarsdale. I could see a handful of Rob's old friends gathering by the steps, a frigid gust whipping their ties over their shoulders. They just wanted to get the funeral service over with.

"Read the eulogy, Craig," she said, placing the palm of her hand over mine. I thought it felt a little moist, a sure sign that she was hiding something again: sweaty hands.

"Sure," I said, moving my hand away and picking up the piece of paper. "Why not? Just for laughs."

"I'm listening."

"I don't know where to begin," I said. "I guess I could tell you the story of two brothers who were the worst of enemies. Who did things to each other that will never be forgotten . . ."

I stopped for a moment, clicked the pen with my thumb.

"Finish it," she said. She was loosely touching the handle of a coffee cup. The purple rim around it, a healing bruise.

"I think I need to explain how we were driving back toward him. Right before he jumped off that bridge. What was that river called again? The details are important."

"What are you talking about, Craig?" she asked, a tear forming in her right eye.

I couldn't help myself. One thing I'd never fall for is the bridge trick. It bothered me that he thought so little of me that he was trying for death twice in a row.

Rebecca stared back at me.

"Why would he jump?" I asked her.

"We keep going over this," she said. "He thought I was leaving him."

"But what if he didn't?"

"Craig. This isn't a joke. We're about to fucking bury him."

"Are you in on it? I mean, I already know. I just want to hear you say it."

She was looking at me as if I was crazy, but I still couldn't say for sure that we were burying my brother. I'd seen his body at the funeral home. I'd even touched his stiff, embalmed chest, stony underneath the shirt. But then I'd taken a step back, feeling something greasy on my fingers. The body could have been meticulously shaped out of wax. It was entirely possible, I thought, that this was the best turn he'd ever take. And then I was sure. That wasn't him. He could have paid thousands to have this thing created that was lying in the coffin. Or maybe he'd even come up with a way to temporarily render himself unconscious.

I imagined my brother falling off the bridge as I spoke to her then. It was just a beautiful trick. He'd hidden behind the railing and thrown something heavy off the bridge as we came driving toward him. He could have crouched and run to the Foxburg side of the bridge as we stopped on it. He could have hidden in the forest. He might be in contact with Rebecca. It was my turn, that was all I knew. And I wanted this one more than ever. My wife was dead. Jerome was too.

The fact that I had been cleared of any wrongdoing was irrelevant. All I had was the game now, and temporary possession of Rebecca Krider. Because he was coming back for her.

I knew I had to be careful. He was thinking one step ahead. One step beyond my next move. That was always allowed. And he hadn't wound up killing me, and I hadn't killed him. So my father's three rules were still technically intact.

The game was still on.

"It's my turn," I said to her.

"You sound like a child," she said, looking out the window. "There are no more turns. You won. Is that what you want?"

I'd have to hire someone to watch her, I thought to myself. I'd have to put spyware on everything she used.

"I'll find him," I said. "I'll track him down, wherever he is. I know he's watching us."

I waved out the window of the diner, just to let him know.

"You're losing it," she said.

Or I'd have to have her killed, I thought, looking at her. She might go to the police, despite how much she feared me. Her face looked pale, the makeup dusty in the winter sunlight. I'd kissed her in the car and she'd barely parted her lips.

"We need to talk about a Plan B," I said. "In case he decided the rules don't apply anymore. In case he has a fucking sharpshooter out there. I need a backup emergency plan at all times. I need to know that things get taken care of, even if I'm gone."

"There's no Plan B," she said, standing up. "He's dead. He's lying in the church right now. We should go."

The mourners were arranging their ties again, guiding their wives into the church a little early, tenderly touching the small of their backs. It was too cold for small talk. Everyone wanted to get it over with, everyone but me.

"Rebecca," I said. "You two were a pretty good team. I've got to admit that. But we're going to be even better."

I stood up, calmly pushed the chair back underneath the table, and left her there. I thought I had seen something deep in the bare branches of the trees across the road. Movement. A dark color. Something like a flash.

I pushed open the door and walked down the sidewalk, shielding my eyes against the cold blot of winter sun, staring at the trees. Whatever I thought I had seen had vanished for now.

Turning slowly back toward the coffee shop, I waited for her, taking a deep breath, telling myself to be patient as she finally opened the door and walked toward me.

She turned around suddenly as if someone had called her name, was playing games with her.

"Rebecca!" I said, irritably shoving my hand in my jacket pocket, touching the piece of paper there. I took it out and unfolded it. From the other side of the street, Rebecca was carefully watching me, smiling for the first time in weeks, watching me read his old bloodstained toast. I'd saved it. I would save it until I saw him again.

It was my turn, and I was going to savor every minute. I couldn't wait to see his face again, and I knew I would. I just had to be patient. It was just a matter of time.

■

In the church, I took my place with Rebecca in the first pew. There might have been twenty people there at best. Some squat woman in a hideous blue pantsuit was plinking away on a classical guitar. "Let It Be." A song Rob used to come up with creepy alternate lyrics to when we were young. "In my hour of darkness, Mother Mary bleeds for me. . . ."

I could hear my mother weeping behind me. That persistent nonentity. I think she wanted me to turn around and see what a mess her face was. I think she wanted a hug. After all this time, you'd think I could have just turned around and done that.

But I was looking at my brother's coffin. Three fake-looking lilies gleaming right in the center. The priest, who had been sitting in a chair, smiling at all of us as we'd filed in, was standing. He was adjusting the tiny microphone at the lectern.

"Welcome," he said, spreading his hands wide and then slowly bringing them together.

I felt like I was going to explode laughing. I held my hand against my mouth, swallowed the pricelessness of it all, and then turned to Rebecca.

"C'mon, where is he?" I said.

She shook her head and stared straight forward at the priest.

I wanted to step into the aisle. I wanted to open his coffin again. I wanted to show them all that this was just another beginning.

"How much is he paying these people?" I whispered to her, too loudly. Looking over my shoulder, I glanced at a few of them. They could have been anybody. They probably each had little backstories they'd painstakingly been paid to memorize, but after the service I'd find a way to trip them up.

■

But first things first, I had to practice the speech I was about to give. I closed my eyes and whispered the words softly.

"I don't know where to begin," I repeated, closing my eyes and reciting the words. "I guess I could tell you the story of two brothers."

I took Rebecca's hand and held it tightly, maybe too tightly. She turned to me, and I wondered how she could look at me like that. As if she cared deeply about me. As if, at that exact moment, she really wanted me to believe my brother was dead. I'd been waiting for her to look at me like that for years, and now all I could do was pray she'd keep holding my hand so I didn't make a fool of myself. There are times when it all becomes too much. The game is worse than the world caving in.

I took a deep breath. I narrowed my eyes as if I were looking through a rifle scope and watched the priest spread his arms again.

EPILOGUE

"Come here," the boy said.

"We just started," the girl said.

"Give me another kiss."

She stopped just long enough for him to catch up to her, and then she ran away again. He could catch her and hold her, but they had all day. The thought of being with her all day makes him so happy he's almost ashamed. She could really hurt him now if she dumped him, and they've only known each other since June.

It's an easy trail, but he wishes he'd picked a better hotel. The wineglass had a lipstick smudge on it. One of the guests, a man actually wearing a leisure suit, tried to hit on her when he was signing up for bocce ball.

It was better out here, walking behind her, running after her when she wasn't looking and then watching her jog ahead of him again. She had a silly way of running, arms held high in the air.

"Better watch out for snakes," he said.

"That's not funny," she said, turning toward him and staring at him with mock anger.

"I see one right there," he said, stealing up to her, only a few feet away now. He's going to kiss her again. It's the perfect place. No hotel guests gossiping about how young they were because they didn't have anything else to talk about.

She ran away again, and for a moment he just watched her, knowing that the next time she stopped she'd wait for him, hold out her arms and wrap them around him and let him kiss her neck. He could imagine her shrieking playfully when he placed his cold hands underneath her sweater.

They've lost the trail, but he wasn't worried. There wasn't much of a trail there to begin with. He guessed most of the guests were too old to be interested in walking through these woods anyway. It won't be hard to find their way back. He could hear a tennis ball being hit on the clay court back at the resort. A reassuring hollow pop, so they must still be close.

Up ahead, he could see a bit of faded white siding, suddenly visible through the trees. A house. He hears a man's voice in the distance.

She's standing still. She's smiling, but not at him. She's looking upwards, into the trees, and she's waving.

ACKNOWLEDGEMENTS

I'd like to thank the wonderful team at Adaptive, Matt Wise, Kate Imel, and Colby Groves, for their insights and enthusiasm.